I0566104

Of Course He Pushed Him
& Other Sherlock Holmes Stories

Volume One: Traditional Sherlock Holmes Pastiches

By

Chris Chan

Edited by David Marcum and Derrick Belanger

First edition published in 2022
© Copyright 2022
Chris Chan

The right of Chris Chan to be identified as the author of this work has been asserted by him in accordance with the Copyright, Designs and Patents Act 1998.

All rights reserved. No reproduction, copy or transmission of this publication may be made without express prior written permission. No paragraph of this publication may be reproduced, copied or transmitted except with express prior written permission or in accordance with the provisions of the Copyright Act 1956 (as amended). Any person who commits any unauthorised act in relation to this publication may be liable to criminal prosecution and civil claims for damage.

All characters appearing in this work are fictitious. Any resemblance to real persons, living or dead, is purely coincidental. The opinions expressed herein are those of the author and not of MX Publishing.

Paperback ISBN 978-1-80424-057-1
ePub ISBN 978-1-80424-058-8
PDF ISBN 978-1-80424-059-5

Published by MX Publishing
335 Princess Park Manor, Royal Drive,
London, N11 3GX
www.mxpublishing.co.uk

Cover design by Brian Belanger

List of Original Publication Dates and Venues

"The Bitter Gravestones," published in *The MX Book of New Sherlock Holmes Stories, Part XXX: More Christmas Adventures (1897-1928)*, edited by David Marcum, MX Publishing (November 2021).

"The Diogenes Club Poltergeist," published in *The MX Book of New Sherlock Holmes Stories, Vol. XVII: Stranger than Fiction*, edited by David Marcum , MX Publishing (October 2019).

"The Heinous Half-Crowns," published in *Beyond the Adventures of Sherlock Holmes, Volume Three*, edited by Brian and Derrick Belanger, Belanger Books (December 2020).

"Intruders at Baker Street," published in *The MX Book of New Sherlock Holmes Stories, Part XXII: Some More Untold Cases 1877-1887*, edited by David Marcum, MX Publishing (November 2020).

"The Man in the Maroon Suit," published in *The MX Book of New Sherlock Holmes Stories, Part XIX: 2020 Annual (1882-1890)*, edited by David Marcum, Belanger Books (May 2020).

"Merridew of Abominable Memory," published in *The MX Book of New Sherlock Holmes Stories, Part XXII: Some More Untold Cases 1877-1887*, edited by David Marcum, MX Publishing (November 2020).

"The Switched String," published in *The MX Book of New Sherlock Holmes Stories, Part XXV: 2021 Annual (1881-1888)*, edited by David Marcum, MX Publishing (May 2021).

Once more, to my parents, Drs. Carlyle and Patricia Chan

And to my USM escape room friends, who did so much to keep my spirits up during the pandemic:

Anjail Floyd-Pruitt

James Grossman

Bill Lent

Blake Wanger

Contents

Introduction

Volume One: Traditional Sherlock Holmes Pastiches

Introduction

Volume One: Traditional Sherlock Holmes Pastiches

Sherlock Holmes has been a part of my life ever since I was a child. I have always loved the movie and television adaptations, the radio plays, and especially, the original stories. However, ever since I was about ten years old, I have been very disappointed in Sir Arthur Conan Doyle, due to the fact that he got his work so incredibly wrong. By reading a book introduction, I learned that Conan Doyle believed that the Sherlock Holmes stories were beneath him, and he had grown to loathe his detective. I didn't know what had happened to lead such a talented man so horribly astray, but even at the age of ten, I knew that Conan Doyle was horribly, inexplicably misguided. How could a seemingly intelligent fellow come to believe that these wonderful stories weren't worth writing? How could he dislike such a brilliant character as Holmes? To this day, I still don't have a convincing answer to those questions.

A few years ago, I saw an advertisement from Belanger Books asking for submissions to one of their anthologies. They were looking for new Sherlock Holmes stories, and I, having a bit of extra time, decided to try my hand at one. After my first tale was accepted, MX Publishing asked me to submit to another anthology, so I did, and I kept on writing.

Many of these stories were written under a theme. "The Diogenes Club Poltergeist" was for an edition of *The MX Book of New Sherlock Holmes Stories* with the theme "Stranger Than Fiction," a collection of mysteries featuring a crime that at first glance seemed to be connected to the paranormal, but actually weren't. I've always been fascinated by Sherlock's brother Mycroft, as well as his coterie of totally unsociable associates, so I decided to set my story amongst them.

"The Man in the Maroon Suit" wasn't for a themed anthology, but it was inspired in part by seeing some graffiti on a piece of public art. I wondered who would deface something lovely. It gave me an idea, which mutated several times before becoming that story.

"Merridew of Abominable Memory" and "Intruders at Baker Street" (originally titled "The Darlington Substitution") were for an MX anthology with the theme *Some More Untold Cases*, based on references in the original stories to cases that never made their way in full into the canon. I tried to give Mr. Merridew a different spin. Most readers think he was such a horrid man that the memory of him was abominable to all. I decided that maybe he just had a terrible memory. But why was his brain so impaired? As for "Intruders at Baker Street," I remembered thinking after learning that Holmes left 221B to study bees in Sussex, that no one else could really feel like they belonged there. So what might happen if some interlopers were living at 221B when they shouldn't have been?

"The Heinous Half-Crowns" was for a Belanger Books anthology of sequels to the original stories. The bad guys, who were counterfeiters, get away at the end of "The Engineer's Thumb." My story wraps up that dangling thread.

"The Switched String" was for an unthemed MX anthology. I wanted to start with something amiss at 221B. What would happen if someone replaced one of the strings on Holmes' violin? Why would they do such a thing? Therein lies the mystery.

Finally, "The Bitter Gravestones" was for a Christmas-themed MX anthology. My inspiration was a present-day story about some people who had never forgiven their mother for abandoning them when they were children. They wrote and published an obituary outlining her many transgressions that went viral, and finished by saying "She will not be missed." What might happen if somebody had similarly angry comments carved onto headstones? And so, Holmes and Watson investigated some nasty epitaphs at Christmastime.

I hope that all of these stories are as fun to read as they were to write.

–Chris Chan

*Part One: Traditional Sherlock Holmes
Pastiches*

The Diogenes Club Poltergeist

Readers who follow the exploits of Sherlock Holmes and myself will be familiar with the Diogenes Club, that remarkable gathering place for those antisocial men who wish to read quietly in a comfortable chair without having to deal with those most frustrating of creatures: their fellow human beings. Holmes' brother Mycroft is a fixture of that peculiar assemblage of the resolutely unclubbable. Members of the Diogenes Club are strictly forbidden from speaking, and an atmosphere of absolute silence is rigidly imposed within its walls, except in the Stranger's Room. While the majority of men, including myself, might find the values of this club to be utterly alien to their own tastes, the world is composed of every conceivable sort of person, and the members of the Diogenes Club continue to bother no one and insist that no one bother them.

The rigidly enforced peace of the Diogenes Club was shattered one overcast winter's day when Holmes received a telegram from Mycroft at breakfast. He read it, raised an eyebrow, and wordlessly handed it to me. It read:

SHERLOCK–

PAY NO ATTENTION TO THE LETTERS FROM MY FELLOW MEMBERS OF THE DIOGENES CLUB. BURN THEM UNREAD.

–MYCROFT

"Why on earth would Mycroft want you to destroy letters from his fellows at the Diogenes Club?" I wondered. "And how could you possibly know that the letters were from members of the Club without reading them first? Surely you don't know the names of every man who belongs to that bizarre organization?"

"As for your second question, the correspondence of men writing from the Diogenes Club is immediately distinguishable by the club's stationary, which is thicker than the standard envelopes and writing paper, and possesses a distinctive watermark. It's true that I only know a handful of the Diogenes Club's members' names, and at the moment I have no idea why Mycroft would be so anxious for me to avoid reading their correspondence. But if I may point out an important point, Watson, you are missing a much more important question."

"And that would be?"

"Why would members of the Diogenes Club be writing to me in the first place? One of Mycroft's fellows might conceivably choose to consult me about something, but more than one? Surely it is too much to believe that multiple members of that group would simultaneously feel compelled to write to me with different problems? Therefore, they must all be writing about the same issue. Now, there is no link between the club members other than the club itself. They come from all walks of life, and they mostly have no contact whatsoever outside the walls of the Diogenes Club. It follows, then, that there is some problem threatening the sanctity of the Diogenes Club. The members are not in the habit of consulting each other, so multiple members are sending letters of their own initiative, rather than one letter representing the entire group. We can further deduce that the problem is one that involves some crime or mysterious circumstance. If it were some simple matter such as an overly talkative member, they could simply take the normal steps to remove the offender. But if there is a problem that would require my involvement, why would Mycroft request that I stay out of the matter? Normally, Mycroft would jump at the chance at letting me handle such a situation, because his deep-seated indolence would make him resent any call for him to investigate himself. I can only assume that Mycroft considers the problem at hand to be a situation that is unworthy of my modest powers, and that he feels so strongly about the matter that he decided to send me a telegram that would reach me before the morning post."

Holmes' theories were verified less than an hour later, when he received no fewer than nine envelopes which bore the watermark of the Diogenes Club stationery. After rifling through the sealed stack, he declared, "Clearly, Watson, the members of the Diogenes Club are under a great deal of distress."

I knew he was expecting me to respond with an incredulous "How could you possibly know that, Holmes?" Perhaps it was a sudden impulse of recalcitrance, but I refused to provide him with the prompting question he obviously desired. After a few silent moments, Holmes looked up at me with an expression that was both slightly chiding and a gentle plea, and my resolve shattered. Reluctantly, I asked the question I had refrained from posing mere moments earlier.

"Quite simple, my dear fellow. Smell the sealed adhesive on these six envelopes."

I did so. "Brandy. Whiskey. Whiskey again. Beer. More whiskey. Gin."

"Precisely, Watson. The men who composed these letters have been drinking profusely. But the members of the Diogenes Club never drink to excess, at least inside the walls of the building. Overconsumption of alcohol leads to loosened tongues, which leads to conversation, which is exactly what members come to the Diogenes Club to avoid. If six members required several strong drinks to write a letter to me, then something particularly upsetting happened there, something disturbing enough to make previously restrained men succumb to the comforts of the bottle. And I notice some important points on these two that do not smell of alcohol. The penmanship on both envelopes clearly shows the untidiness of a distraught mind. The stamps are askew. The ink has splattered a bit on both of these envelopes, clearly the pens were being held by people in a state of nervous agitation. Of course, the similar ink blots on the other six envelopes further prove that the men who wrote these letters drank to excess."

"Yes, but what is the cause of their distress?"

"That I cannot tell without opening the letters, Watson. And as curious as I am to figure out what is going on, my dear brother has specifically requested that I burn these envelopes unopened, and I would not dream of jeopardizing my relationship with my sibling over something so trifling as curiosity over the contents of some envelopes."

At that moment there was a knock at the door, and Mrs. Hudson entered with a telegram. Holmes tore it open, laughed, and tossed it to me.

SHERLOCK–

ON SECOND THOUGHT, DON'T BURN THE LETTERS. BRING THEM TO ME AS SOON AS YOU GET THEM.

–MYCROFT

"Mycroft certainly enjoys giving you orders," I mused.

"He has no doubt realized what can be deduced from this morning's correspondence, but for once Mycroft is a step behind me. He cannot determine who is behind whatever event is shaking up the Diogenes Club without seeing these envelopes, so I must bring them to him. It should only take Mycroft a few seconds to make the same deduction I did about the identity of the party behind whatever is bothering the members of the club. Let us meet Mycroft at his rooms, Watson, and see what has caused this wave of unrest."

It was not until we were shaking hands with Mycroft in his sitting-room that I realized that Sherlock had failed to explain exactly what in the unopened correspondence he had received was so revelatory. I had no time to ask, however, since Mycroft took control of the conversation before I could speak.

"I heard from my sources that you led the police to make an arrest in the Gunton case," Mycroft told his brother.

"That's correct."

"Did you make the connection to the Barnett garroting from three years ago?"

"I wasn't aware of that case. Remember, I was pretending to be dead at that time. I was on the other end of the world and I was unable to follow the local crime news."

"Of course, of course. You need to have a word with your Scotland Yard friends. I suspect that Malvern may have been involved in both crimes. The signature is identical."

"I shall inform Lestrade to look into that immediately. But you didn't summon me here to talk about the Gunton case. What exactly is happening at the Diogenes Club, dear brother?"

Mycroft groaned and leaned back in his chair. "It's a terrible inconvenience. The calm and quiet of my sanctuary has been shattered. Many members of the club are convinced that there is… a poltergeist disrupting the building."

"Excuse me?" Holmes responded as if he hadn't understood a word Mycroft had said.

"A poltergeist or some such rot. The outlandish belief that some malevolent supernatural being is haunting the Diogenes Club, wreaking havoc and upsetting the members."

"Surely a collection of grown men could not possibly give any credence to such a ridiculous supposition," I scoffed.

Mycroft frowned at me. "You forget, doctor, that the membership of the Diogenes Club is not based upon being skeptical or level-headed. The sole criterions are to dislike unnecessary conversation and to be able to refrain from speaking. Many of the men who populate our membership may well be superstitious and possess a belief in ghoulies and ghosties and long-legged beasties and things that go bump in the night. I wouldn't know. I've never shared two words with the vast majority of our membership, so I have no idea what sort of men they are. Frankly, until now, I've never really cared about their personal thoughts or beliefs, and I hoped that they never extended any curiosity towards mine. Now, I am reluctantly forced to conclude that I am surrounded by hysterics."

Holmes pressed the tips of his fingers together and frowned. "Surely there must be some sort of reasons for this widespread delusion."

"Of course. It's nothing more than a series of practical jokes. Mean-spirited ones, but all easily explainable. Windowpanes, bottles, glasses, vases… anything that's fragile is shattering without apparent cause. The past week, members have been reading their newspapers, only have them catch fire while they were reading them. Members are being pelted with rotten food or splashed with icy cold water while they doze off in their chairs."

"There's absolutely nothing mysterious about that," Holmes scoffed. The broken glass and china? A simple catapult would explain that. The newspapers? A magnifying glass focusing the rays of a light sources. The rotten food? All that would take is an arm with good aim, or perhaps the catapult again."

"What about the ice water?" I asked.

"Any mechanic or engineer could design a simple device shaped like a pistol that sprays a stream of water when you pull the trigger. Or possibly a smaller version of a syringe used to spray pesticide on plants."

"Of course, Sherlock. As expected, your train of thought is following mine precisely. Nothing that occurred cannot be explained by pranks known by any mischievous schoolboy. The mysterious disembodied voices that have been plaguing several members of the club at inopportune times–"

"Ventriloquism."

"Obviously. But a number of club members– and some members of the staff– insist that they've actually seen the poltergeist."

"Really? What does it look like?"

"Eyewitness descriptions disagree, which is not surprising. They all agree that the supposed poltergeist can fly, and that an unearthly glow emanates from it. But after that point, the witnesses' testimony differs. Some people claim that it has a massive tail, others say three heads, others say enormous wings, or bright red eyes. No two descriptions match."

"How long has the poltergeist been active?"

"Just under a week. But the damage it has done to the club is incalculable."

I seized this opportunity to reenter the conversation. "You mean the physical harm caused by the destruction?"

"No, Watson! The noise! Because due to all of the disruption, all of the chaos, the unthinkable has happened. Members of the club are actually… *talking to each other*. The Stranger's Room is filled to bursting with club members chatting, sharing their experiences being pestered by the poltergeist and their personal theories about its origins and what it's trying to accomplish with its hijinks. And the members of the club of carrying on their conversations elsewhere! They are interacting with each other socially and even forming the beginnings of friendships!"

I attempted to keep my voice level. "And how does that pose a danger to the Diogenes Club?"

From the look on his face, Mycroft's evaluation of my mental powers had never been lower. "It means the end of all we stand for! If a majority of the members of the club petition to amend the rules so they can spend time together, they will destroy the spirit and purpose of the Diogenes Club. The Diogenes Club as we know it will cease to exist! It will become a place of socializing, just like any other club in London!"

I realized that it would not be a wise decision to voice the thoughts that were currently running through my mind, and I worried that my facial expression would produce a similar effect to the one that I sought to avoid, so I rose with a quiet "excuse me" and crossed over to the window. Mycroft's well-known aversion towards moving longer distances than necessary played a pivotal role in his selection of the building across the street from his personal rooms as the site of the Diogenes Club. As I looked through the window and stared at the building across the street, I mentally noted how undistinctive it was, noting that there was no sign identifying its purpose. Had I not known what was inside its walls, I would have walked past the building without a second thought, and had anybody asked me to take a guess as the structure's use, I would have been left at a complete loss.

I was brought out of my meditations by the sound of shattering glass, followed by the sight of a man falling out of a top-story window of the Diogenes Club. As he fell, I saw a small object with an eerie green glow flying out the window, zigzagging through the air, and zooming away out of my line of sight.

Immediate action was clearly necessary. "Holmes! Mycroft!" I rapidly explained the situation as I bolted out of Mycroft's flat and sprinted down the stairs. Holmes was right behind me. Though I couldn't see him, I knew that if he did choose to follow us, Mycroft would be proceeding at a much slower pace.

I had neither enough time nor enough breath to tell Holmes what I had seen. Within moments, I was examining the man who had just defenestrated from the club. Fortunately, the building was not particularly tall, and the man had struck a fairly leafy tree on the way down, which had destroyed several branches, but had also slowed his rate of falling enough so as to substantially reduce the risk of fatal damage. After a basic check of his limbs, it was clear that both of his legs and his right arm were broken, though mercifully there did not seem to be any damage to his head.

The poor man was clearly suffering from shock. I gently leaned over him until I could make direct eye contact with him. "Sir, if you can hear me, you have sustained some serious injuries, but at the moment I do not believe that they will be life-threatening, nor will they be permanently debilitating." The injured man did not reply, but his eyes latched onto my gaze, so I concluded that he could hear me. "Can you tell me what happened to you? Why did you fall out the window? Did you jump or were you pushed?" That was probably more questions than I ought to have asked, but I was rather shaken from what I had just seen, and my bedside manner probably needed a little refinement.

The injured man blinked a few times and then sighed very softly. I crouched over him for a little over half a minute, until finally he spoke.

"The... polt... er... geist..." After these two words, his voice trailed away and his eyes broke contact with mine.

"Will he be all right?" Holmes abruptly reminded me of his presence, causing me to start involuntarily.

"He's passed out, but he'll live and most likely recover after a lengthy period of convalescence."

"I have summoned an ambulance, but it will be some time before it arrives. How are you feeling? Will you need a drop of brandy in order to recover yourself?"

My first instinct was to happily accept, but I immediately remembered that I still had a patient that needed my attention, and when the ambulance arrived I wanted to explain the injured man's condition without liquor on my breath. After I politely declined, Holmes took a moment to direct the gathering crowd to stand back further. Having finished, he leaned over to me and asked, "As you were running out of Mycroft's rooms, you mumbled something about a green glow. Would you mind explaining what you meant, please?"

I nodded, and rapidly informed Holmes of the flying object with the unearthly aura that sailed out the window and into the street. "I've no idea what it was, Holmes. I'm quite certain that it wasn't really a poltergeist or any other paranormal creature, but for the life of me I couldn't possibly tell you what it really was."

I was grateful to observe that there was no incredulity or judgment in Holmes' face. He listened my eyewitness account, nodded, thanked me, and immediately left the scene, returning a little under five minutes later.

"Where did you go?" I asked.

"I summoned some much-needed assistance. Have you determined this injured man's identity?"

With a bit of self-reproach, I confessed that I hadn't checked his wallet or searched for any other form of identification.

"I can save you the trouble," Mycroft's voice boomed from behind me. "His name is Rufus Darbington, and he is one of the men who sent you a letter." Mycroft turned to Holmes. "Before this happened, you were about to show me the correspondence you received today. May I please see it now?"

Holmes swiftly withdrew the stack of envelopes from his pocket and passed it to his brother. Mycroft grunted something that I

15

could only assume was an expression of thanks, and he rifled through the sealed correspondence, squinted at the writing on each one, and sniffed each envelope in turn.

"Darbington's is the one that smells of gin," Mycroft proclaimed. "He is very fond of some bizarre concoction known as a martini. He has been drinking a great many of them the last few days."

"Now that you have had a few seconds to examine the evidence, no doubt you have arrived at the same deductions that I have," Holmes commented.

"Of course. I suspected him from the beginning, of course, but his letter confirms it."

I felt the need to re-insert myself into this conversation. "Excuse me please, but what are you two talking about?"

"We will explain everything in a moment, Watson. The ambulance is arriving. As soon as this man is safely on the way to hospital, the three of us will– Mycroft, should we meet inside the Stranger's Room or your own flat?"

"My flat, I think. We can be assured of utter privacy and no ears to the keyholes there."

The moment the three of us were securely ensconced in Mycroft's comfortable chairs, Holmes began explaining everything to me.

"I realize that you did not get a chance to examine the letters I received this morning, but I believe that I described them sufficiently enough for you to figure out *which* was the notable one, even if you could not possibly know *who* is the person who is currently our most prominent person of interest."

"And you haven't even opened the letters yet!"

"True, and it's certainly possible that there may be useful information inside of them. But use your powers of memory, Watson. Describe what you know of the letters."

I cast my mind back. "Nine letters. Six of them smell of various kinds of alcohol. I believe that at least one smelled of whiskey–"

"For the moment, the types of alcohol consumed by those who licked the envelopes are irrelevant. What else?"

"Two more did not smell of alcohol, but the writing was sloppy and the stamps askew. The liquor-scented ones were messy as well."

"Precisely! Which leads to which important point?"

"Six plus two is eight. What of the ninth envelope?"

"Capital, dear fellow, capital! Of the nine envelopes sent to me today, only one was addressed in neat handwriting and did not smell of alcohol. I hasten to add that several of the envelopes that smelled of liquor also had messy handwriting on them. Clearly, the men who wrote the letters were distraught. It showed in their shaking hands in their excessive consumption of spirits. But one man sent me a letter that did not betray any signs of distress. What does that mean to you?"

I took a breath and pondered my answer for a moment. "It means that the person who wrote the ninth letter was not upset like his colleagues were. It might be concluded that he is simply a preternaturally calm and unflappable person, or at least does a better job of disguising his distress from the world. But it might also imply a more sinister motive. This man may not be visibly nervous because he knows for a fact that he has nothing to be worried about, which would only be the case if..." I realized that I was pausing for dramatic effect, and silently I chastised myself for doing so. "Maybe, he knows the true facts behind the appearance of this supposed poltergeist. Perhaps he's the hoaxer who has been playing the unexpected pranks. I do not know for certain, but I perhaps the whole reason for writing a letter was to deflect suspicion. This was a miscalculation, because you and your brother were wary immediately."

Holmes laughed and his eyes twinkled with delight. "Don't forget to include yourself along with Mycroft and myself. It fooled none of us."

"I do have one more question, Holmes."

"And that, no doubt, is "Whose name is on the suspicious envelope?"" With a smile, Holmes once again removed the stack of correspondence from his pocket and handed me the top envelope.

Reading aloud, I declared, "Ian Dynell."

"What do you know of him, Mycroft? I realize that the nature of the Diogenes Club makes it unlikely that you would ever have a lengthy conversation– or even a short one– with him, but surely you would have done some research regarding his background before admitting him to membership?"

"I know precious little of Mr. Dynell, other than the fact that he is a solicitor's clerk, he's married with four energetic children, that his wife is very fond of talking, and they live with his wife's extremely opinionated mother."

"That explains why he might seek out the solace of the Diogenes Club."

"Indeed. I was surprised that he could afford the membership fees, as the well-worn state of his suit made it clear that he was a man of limited income."

"How long has he been a member?"

"A little under a month. Only a few weeks, in fact. He's the most recently inducted member of the club."

I could not help myself from asking a question, even though I was certain that I already knew the answer. "Is there any sort of initiation ceremony for new members?"

Mycroft stared at me as if I'd asked him to knit a sweater for an elephant. "Of course not! In fact, one of the questions we ask prospective members is what they'd like us to serve at their welcoming banquet. If they fail to recoil in horror at the prospect of an evening of socializing, or if they don't ask if they can eat their banquet dinner alone or something like that, we know at once that they are not Diogenes Club material, and we deny their application for membership at once."

All I could manage was a very small nod.

"Perhaps we can speak to Mr. Dynell now," Holmes said. "Do you know where he would be right now?"

"There's a chance that he's at the Diogenes Club right now. He's been in the habit of eating an early lunch at the club most weekday afternoons, and then returning at some point in the evening."

"Then may I suggest that the three of cross the street to question him? Normally I would not wish to disturb you, dear brother, but your presence will assure our entry."

As we entered the club, I noticed that there was no sign of the police, and mentioned the fact.

"There's no reason why they should be here," Mycroft replied. "None of the members want the authorities tramping about our sanctuary and asking impertinent questions. Besides, the members are well trained in scrupulously ignoring their fellows. I wouldn't be surprised if everybody simply failed to notice Darbington falling out the window. Now, remember the rules of the club. No more talking from this point on, please. If you absolutely must communicate, use these pads of paper and pencils." Mycroft took those items from a pair of baskets on a nearby table and then handed them to us.

Holmes immediately began scribbling. "Shall we investigate the dining room?"

Mycroft did not bother writing a reply. He simply nodded and gestured towards a pair of large oak doors. As we passed through them, we saw a couple of elderly gentlemen sitting at a table and drinking. Both looked like they'd already imbibed well past the point of propriety, especially it being so early in the day. Mycroft wrinkled his nose, as if it was positively abhorrent to him to see two club members sitting in such close proximity to each other, even if they were not speaking a single word.

Holmes' pencil flew across his pad of paper and showed it to us. "These are Grove and Quarles, I presume?"

Mycroft nodded.

"How did you know their names?" I wrote.

Holmes replied by scrawling, "The men are clearly unnerved and using alcohol to steady their nerves. Clearly the type of men who would write to me to investigate a supposed poltergeist at their club. The ink stains on their right hands matching the ink on the letters further supports my conclusions. You will note that Grove is drinking brandy and Quarles is gulping down beer. I matched them to the names on the alcoholic odors on the envelopes. Simplicity itself."

Mycroft pointed a large finger at a table in the corner. No one was seated at it, but there was a glass of water and a large bowl of some lumpy beef soup upon it on it. The bowl was only half full, and a great deal of the muddy-looking brown broth had spilled over all the floor-length white tablecloth. Holmes crossed over, examined the aforementioned items, as well as the saltcellar, the napkin, fork, and spoon on the table, and frowned.

"What's missing, Watson?" he wrote.

"The man eating this food?" I scribbled back.

"True, but what else?"

After two more seconds, I had it. "Where's the knife?" I wrote.

Holmes nodded and looked thoughtfully at the table, and then lifted up the long white tablecloth that reached the floor. Underneath it was a very dead body with a table knife sticking in its throat. I took a moment to confirm that life was extinct, then got up to look at what Holmes was writing to Mycroft.

"Dynell?"

Mycroft nodded.

"We shall have to summon the police now." Holmes scribbled.

"Nonsense. It's clear who did this. You just need to find the proof, and the police should be satisfied. They won't ask the club members any impertinent questions then."

"I just need to find the proof?"

"Well you don't expect me to investigate, do you?"

I joined the silent conversation, writing, "How can you possibly know who did this?"

"Look at what's next to the body."

As soon as I read Holmes' note, I noticed a large, bloodstained white napkin lying on the ground beside the corpse.

"The sort of cloth worn by a waiter over his arm while serving. Dynell was stabbed by his own waiter while he ate, and the waiter used the cloth to protect himself from being spattered with blood."

"You can't be sure of that. There are a hundred–"

Holmes didn't let me finish writing. "A quick investigation will prove it."

Grove and Quarles were still drinking silently. "Shouldn't we question them? They could be witnesses?"

Mycroft dismissed my idea. "Useless. Diogenes Club members take no notice of each other, alive or dead. When Major Strausser had his fatal heart attack last fall in a library armchair, it was five days before the smell alerted his fellow clubmen to the fact."

I was finding not being able to use my voice to be increasingly frustrating. "Can I please start talking now? I'm running out of paper and the lead is wearing out on my pencil."

"Certainly not." Mycroft wrote that two-word note with such authority that I didn't have it in me to question it.

Holmes crossed the room and opened a door, causing the sound of kitchen noises and the odors of cooking to fill the air. He motioned to the two of us, and we followed him inside. A chef was calmly chopping vegetables.

Holmes scribbled another note and passed it to Mycroft, who nodded. Holmes then showed it to me, so I could see that it read, "Where are the waiters?" Holmes then showed the note to the chef.

The chef wiped his brow with the back of his hand and glared at Holmes. "Listen, gov. I know the rule about not talking in the club, but this is my kitchen and I set the rules. I can't write little notes when I'm filleting fish, can I? If you have a question for me, you can use your bloody voice."

"Very well," Holmes pocketed his notepad and pencil. "What is the name of your waiter, how long has he been working here, and where is he now?"

"His name's Canterville, he's been here for about a week because he's filling in for our regular waiter who's been ill, and he stepped out for a smoke."

"How long ago has it been since you've seen him?"

The chef's forehead creased. "Quite some time, come to think of it. At least ten minutes. Maybe fifteen."

"He won't be coming back." Holmes turned to Mycroft. "There's nothing for it now. I suggest that you bite the bullet and summon the police."

Mycroft made a sour face and took a spoonful of Lancashire hotpot from a casserole dish, presumably in order to comfort himself. "Very well. I shall not call for your friends Lestrade or Gregson, though. I happen to know an inspector who I can trust to be completely discreet and keep inconvenient questions to a minimum."

"It does not matter to me who you tell at Scotland Yard, Mycroft, only that you begin the search for this waiter. This supposed poltergeist is no simple prank. It is part of a far more dangerous and sinister plan."

I need not explain the events of the next hour. When the inspector Mycroft referred to earlier arrived, I was struck by the fact that I had never before met an officer of the law so disinclined to assert his authority. The man was completely obsequious to Mycroft, and accepted Mycroft's suggestions as to how to track the missing man down without question.

After the inspector left, the three of us settled in the Stranger's Room. I initiated the conversation by asking, "What do you intend to do to catch that waiter Canterville?"

"We have already done everything we ought to do, Watson. The official police are far more suited to a major manhunt than a private detective. They have the funds, the time, and the inclination to catch a killer who is almost certainly not named Canterville."

"What makes you so sure that it's an alias?" I asked.

"Perhaps you haven't read it, but there is a popular novella by Oscar Wilde titled *The Canterville Ghost*. I dare say that when our perpetrator applied for the job as a waiter, he consciously or unconsciously used a reference to a paranormal tale when planning a plot about a fake poltergeist."

"But what was the purpose of the whole charade? Simply to annoy the members of the Diogenes Club?"

"Oh, no, Watson, I'm convinced it was far more sinister than that. I must admit that I have only a fair guess at what the culprit's endgame was, though I can take some solace in the fact that brother

Mycroft clearly has a better idea of the motive, judging from his posture."

Mycroft grunted in reply, then gave a tiny nod.

"Think less about the action– creating a fake poltergeist– and focus more on the consequences of the action, Watson."

"Many members of the Diogenes Club were scared."

"True, but that was not the main desired consequence, Watson. The ultimate goal was more than merely spooking the gullible. Consider what happened."

I pondered for a moment. "The Diogenes Club ceased to be a sanctuary for men seeking peace and quiet."

"Precisely dear fellow! Exactly!" Holmes beamed. "So what does that mean?"

"That members would be less likely to visit the club."

"Magnificent! And the desired result of that would be?"

I hesitated. "Fewer members would lead to reduced payment of dues. That would lead to financial problems for the club, which could conceivably lead to the eventual closure of the club and the sale of the building. Could this whole charade have been driven by someone's desire to purchase the property?"

Holmes folded his fingers together. "An intriguing theory, Watson, but given the fact that the members pay annual dues, it would be months and months before the club would be short on funds."

"In any case, some of the club's members are sufficiently wealthy and dependent on the Diogenes Club as a refuge that they would gladly donate the necessary funds to keep it afloat in times of financial need," Mycroft added.

At that moment, the dour concierge of the club entered the room, placed a salver with a pile of glowing matter and a note on the table next to Holmes, and shuffled away. I thought that he was far too dedicated to the club's theme of silence. It was only later that I learned that he was a lifelong mute.

"Aha! My resourceful band of street urchins have managed to track down the object in question." Holmes held up the salver. "Behold the remains of the Diogenes Club poltergeist, Watson."

"What is that?"

"A form of rubber balloon, decorated with bits of glue and rubber to give it the appearance of a ghoul, and then painted with phosphorescent paint. The device was blown up, then released, causing it to fly around the room, making a shrieking noise as air escaped. A nervous person like Darbington could be startled by it to the point that he may have accidentally fallen from a window in a panicked desire to escape from it. Our culprit never expected that to happen. No, Darbington's injuries were not part of any plan. Neither was the balloon posing as a poltergeist planned to sail out of the broken window. Darbington's fall was a doubly tragic accident, because not only was the poor man injured, but Canterville, the mastermind of this plan, realized that his confederate Dynell was shaken up by the injury. I am quite sure that Canterville paid for Dynell's membership dues so that Dynell would serve as his assistant with the various pranks. Canterville himself took the role of a waiter so as to maintain an even lower profile. Perhaps his predecessor was paid off to feign sickness, perhaps he was mildly poisoned so as to give Canterville a chance to take over the job. Diogenes Club members make a point of ignoring each other. They even more studiously ignore waiters. Dynell was guilt-striken over Darbington's injuries, doubtless wished to confess, and Canterville silenced him."

Holmes coughed, then continued. "You wondered, Watson, why I suspected a waiter. I was not inclined to write down my suspicions at that time, but I noticed numerous minute traces of phosphorescent paint on dozens of items in the dining room, such as eating utensils, saltcellars, candleholders, and napkin rings. I already suspected the use of a glowing device to simulate a poltergeist, and logically, a quantity of that paint would stick to the culprit's fingers. Who else would touch all of those items but a waiter? That is how I knew who was behind these disruptions."

Turning to his brother, Holmes asked, "So, Mycroft, why exactly was our man Canterville trying to empty out the Diogenes Club of its members? Surely he was up to some skullduggery where it would be in his interests to have as few potential witnesses as possible. And nothing of note ever happens within these walls. I remembered a case where a man was drawn away from his place of business so a couple of scoundrels could dig in his basement to rob the bank next door. Could a similar principle be in play here? There is no bank next to the Diogenes Club. The only neighboring location of note is… your flat, dear brother."

"Precisely," Mycroft replied. "I'm in the middle of some tricky negotiations with a representative of a foreign government. In a few days, he is coming to my rooms for a secret meeting. I recently received some intelligence telling me that a trained assassin might be trying to strike my guest. I believe that Canterville is that assassin, and he planned to empty out the Diogenes Club so he could prepare for a strike. He wouldn't know the exact time of the meeting, but he could set up his rifle in the largely deserted building, and be prepared to take out the ambassador." Mycroft gave a little sniff that sounded suspiciously like a chuckle. "Little did he know that I have already taken precautions to protect my guest and myself. All of the windows and walls in my flat are bulletproof. This whole charade was laughably misguided from the beginning."

There is little more to tell. Darbington made a full recovery, aside from a slight limp in his left leg. Members of the club managed to take up a collection for Dynell's widow and children without saying a single word, and they easily raised enough to keep the Dynell family comfortable for several years. The man we knew as Canterville was captured and arrested the next morning, and Mycroft's meeting passed without incident.

Within a month, everything returned to normal at the Diogenes Club. Mycroft's fears that the members would begin forging amicable and talkative friendships proved unfounded. As the members who had been severely shaken by the antics of the "poltergeist" began to converse with each other, they overwhelmingly realized that they didn't really enjoy each other's company very much. The status quo of the Diogenes Club members ignoring each other was restored.

Holmes kept the "poltergeist" balloon, inflated it, and hung it in our rooms at Baker Street. "It is a reminder, Watson, that the unscrupulous can manipulate others with the possibility of the paranormal. We must remember not to dismiss the supernatural out of hand, but to thoroughly investigate such claims in order to determine if there is a more prosaic explanation."

The Man in the Maroon Suit

"That sounds delicious to me, Watson. I shall also order the mulligatawny soup and curried lamb at dinner tonight."

"Capital!" I said with a smile. Immediately, my muscles stiffened, as I realized that my friend had performed one of his trademark performances, where he had managed to read my mind without my speaking a word.

I resolved not to give him the satisfaction of asking him how he had managed to follow my thought processes this time. Holmes sat in his chair, staring at me with an amused smile on his lips, pressing his fingerprints together, until I finally broke my silence. I thought I had managed to hold out for at least ten minutes, but a glance at the clock told me I'd managed to stay quiet for only twenty seconds.

"How did you do it, Holmes?" Holmes and I said simultaneously.

My friend allowed himself a little chuckle, and replied, "Quite simple, Watson. I noticed you rubbing your stomach a minute ago, a sure sign that your gastric juices are informing you that your body needs sustenance sooner rather than later. We have, of course, already made reservations at Wilton's at seven-thirty tonight. You are a frequent patron of that establishment– I believe that you have eaten there no fewer than seven times in the past two months. Therefore, you ought to be familiar with their menu and have determined which dishes rank as your favorites."

Holmes paused, either to take a breath or for dramatic effect. I suppose he was only silent for a couple of seconds, but I am embarrassed to say that my impatience got the better of me, and I found myself asking rather louder than I had any right to, "But how did you know what I wished to order?"

"Quite simple, Watson. I notice you running your hand over the wound caused by the Jezail bullet. You were not wincing, as you do when your war injury causes you pain. Therefore, you were reminiscing, which causes you to unconsciously touch your scarred limb. You developed a fondness for curries and other southern Asian foods during your time in Afghanistan. I next saw you looking down on the right lapel of your suit and examining it between thumb and forefinger. Three weeks ago you permanently stained your tan suit when you dribbled mulligatawny– one of your favorite starters– on your right lapel. I therefore calculated that you were determined to partake of a beloved food, but this time you would take special care to protect your clothing from spills. As for the lamb curry, I suspected that you would continue to dine upon foods of southern Asian origin, and then I saw your gaze light upon the fleecy quilt that Mrs. Hudson crocheted for you last Christmas. Soft, white, and woolly, I daresay it made you think of a sheep. I tie the threads together, and I concluded that you had developed a craving for lamb curry. Simple, of course."

"Of course," I replied, not meaning to include sarcasm or asperity in my tone, but realizing that I might have inserted a touch of those unpleasant attributes into my voice inadvertently. Holmes, thankfully, displayed no offense over how I enunciated my words.

Later that evening, Holmes and I were enjoying our meals at Wilton's. I had carefully draped a large napkin over the front of my clothing in order to preserve my suit from being damaged by the mulligatawny. I had recently lost rather more money than I care to admit in a card game, and my budget for sartorial matters was completely wiped out for the foreseeable future. My current wardrobe would have to last me for some time, and I was grateful to Holmes for treating me to dinner that night.

I had just carefully and neatly deposited the final spoonful of mulligatawny into my mouth when a young man wearing a perfectly pressed suit and sporting a shock of dark curly hair that probably hadn't been combed in weeks rushed forward to our table, carrying a chair. He set down the chair with a heavy thud between Holmes and myself, and turned to us both with a desperate look on his face.

"Mr. Holmes, Dr. Watson. My name is Ernest Townshore. Please forgive me for interrupting your dinner like this, but I'm in a terrible state, and I didn't know what to do, and I was walking down the street trying to make heads or tails of my situation, and when I looked through the window and saw the two of you eating it was like kismet to me. I know that I should have made an appointment to see you both at your lodgings at Baker Street, but I think that if I have to wait to talk to you I might explode."

If I didn't know Holmes as well as I do, I would have sworn that the slight upward twitching of his lips was amusement rather than polite annoyance. "Very well, Mr. Townshore," Holmes said. "I would not like it on my conscience that my desire to have a pleasant, quiet meal with my friend inadvertently led to a case of spontaneous human combustion. Please tell me what's bothering you. And if I may make a suggestion, there is no need to include every single detail. A general sense of your predicament will be sufficient for my investigative needs at present. You will, of course, not mind if we continue to dine while you tell us your problem," Holmes added as the waiter cleared away our soup bowls and replaced them with our lamb curries.

"Yes, of course." Mr. Townshore gulped and tugged at his collar. "The problem, you see, is the man in the maroon suit."

"I beg your pardon?" I asked, my fork unconsciously suspended in the air. "A maroon suit? I don't believe that I've ever seen anybody wearing clothing of that color before."

"Nor have I, Doctor, but he's taken over the gallery."

"Do you know this man's name?" I queried.

"Well… no. You see, he's not a real person, as far as I know. He's a little man wearing a maroon suit and tie. And sometimes a maroon top hat. Not always. I forgot to mention that. I've never seen him before, but over the past three days he's been popping up in most of the pictures in the Sternhull Gallery."

"Popping up in pictures?" I was thoroughly confused. "Is he an actual human being?"

"Well, I don't know if he's a true-to-life representation of a real person, but I don't think I've ever seen him in the flesh myself. I've only seen the little pictures of him that have been added into the paintings."

A glint danced in Holmes' eyes, and I knew at once that he had developed an interest in our unexpected dinner guest's problem. "Some vandal is taking a brush and paint and adding a human figure to the artwork at the gallery?"

"Precisely!" Mr. Townshore produced a small brown paper parcel from under his coat. "Please, take a look!"

Holmes took another bite of curry, and then picked up the parcel gingerly, weighed it in his right hand for a couple of seconds, and then untied the string and neatly unwrapped the brown paper. He examined it for a few moments, and then set it down on the table.

"Not a particularly distinguished work," he finally pronounced. "It's a simple pastoral scene. The kind of art you see on chocolate boxes."

I leaned over and examined the painting. It was a depiction of a small brown cottage in a green field, with several trees along the sides. A little man wearing a maroon suit and hat was leaning against the wall of the cottage. It was rather skillfully done, and if I hadn't known that the figure was not supposed to be there, I would never have guessed that the maroon suit man wasn't supposed to be a part of the painting. Personally, I didn't see anything very wrong or for that matter very right about it, but I have never declared myself to be an art connoisseur. "Who painted this?" I asked.

Mr. Townshore gulped. "I did."

Holmes' face betrayed no embarrassment or contrition for his blunt assessment of Mr. Townshore's work. "I can understand your distress at seeing your work vandalized, Mr. Townshore. Do you have other pictures at the Sternhull Gallery?"

"Yes. Seven of them. And all of them have had that man in the maroon suit added to them."

"How many pictures does the Sternhull Gallery hold in all?"

"I haven't counted.   At an estimate, I'd say around two hundred."

"Have all of those pictures been altered?"

"No. Only about sixty-five of them."

Holmes put down his fork and shot Mr. Townshore a piercing glare. "You didn't count them? Why didn't you take the time to acclimate yourself to the details of the situation before coming to me?"

Mr. Townshore squirmed and had the decency to look shamefaced. "I figured that you could take stock of the situation more effectively than I could."

Holmes' face demonstrated that he could see the justice in this remark, but despite his lingering annoyance, he was still clearly intrigued by this unusual problem. "Are all of the other pictures of the men in the maroon suit the same size?"

"Roughly, yes. Some are a bit bigger or smaller, so the figure's proportionately sized to fit into each picture. None are more than a few inches tall, and it's not always a complete man. In some cases, it's just the top half of him sticking out from behind a tree, or just his face and maroon top hat looking in the window. In one, he's swimming– fully clothed– in a pond, in another he's sitting on a rock or talking with people who were already in the painting."

"Do you recognize his face?" I asked.

"No. I've never seen the man before in my life."

Holmes resumed the questioning. "Have there been any threats to the gallery? Any attempts at vandalism?"

"None that I know of."

"Are the paintings permanently defaced?"

"Well, as far as I can tell all of the images of the maroon suit man are in oil-based paint. I suppose that it could be cleaned off by a skilled restorer, but it would take time and probably would cost quite a bit. As I said, the images are all quite small. It would probably be a lot easier for the artists who painted the pictures to simply paint over the man. That's what I plan to do."

"Hmm. Have you spoken to any of the other artists about their defaced work?"

"No. It's only by pure chance that I even found out about the damage. I visited the gallery an hour ago to meet with the owner, Mr. Bradnick. He had a check for me after one of my paintings sold a few days ago. The gallery was closed today, so no one had been there for almost twenty-four hours. Plenty of time for some miscreant to have painted those little men. Anyway, I met Mr. Bradnick at the door, he let me in, and we discovered the vandalism together. I rather lost my grip on things, and before I knew it I was here."

Holmes ran the tip of his finger gently over the painted man in the maroon suit. "How long do you think it would take for a skilled artist to paint one of these men?"

"It's a bit crude. Not very true to life. I suppose that if I were going for speed rather than detail, I could paint one in three or four minutes. No more than five. Less if I fell into the rhythm of reproducing the figure."

"Hmm." The calculations flashed across Holmes' eyes. "With about sixty-five paintings, at three to five minutes per figure, it would take between three and a quarter hours to just under five and a half hours to complete the project. And the gallery was empty was a full day. Plenty of time. And it would take several hours for the figures to dry. This one has no trace of dampness, so whoever painted it didn't do the job too recently." He paused. "How many people would know that the gallery would be empty today?"

"Everybody. It's always closed on Mondays."

"And nobody was supposed to be there at all?"

"Well, Mr. Bradnick sometimes stops by on a Monday for one reason or another. I made the appointment with him to pick up my check around lunchtime today. I've no idea who else might have known about it. I certainly didn't tell anybody."

"No security guard?"

"I don't believe so, no."

"No cleaning staff?"

"Oh…" Mr. Townshore closed his eyes and thought for a few moments. "There is a charwoman who comes by a few times a week to dust and mop the floors. I don't know her very well, but I am aware that Mr. Bradnick trusts her completely. He gave her a key to the gallery, and she comes by when she has a spare evening to do her work. Perhaps she does come in on Mondays. It would make sense. But you don't think that she would do something like this, do you?"

Holmes lifted his shoulders a fraction of an inch. "I haven't got nearly enough information to draw any conclusions at all. I do content that one would need to be a fairly proficient artist in order to paint so many figures so quickly."

"I wonder, Holmes, is it possible that the vandal sought to paint the man in every single picture, but he ran out of time?"

"That's one of many possibilities, Watson. I shall have a better idea of the vandal's motives when I examine the gallery."

Mr. Townshore looked elated. "Then you'll help me?"

"I shall. After I finish my meal, of course. My curry is getting cold. Mr. Townshore, if you wish to order some for yourself, I highly recommend it. I have no intention on rushing as I eat, and you look as if you could use some sustenance in order to regain your composure. Also, I have an eye on a bit of bread and butter pudding for afters."

Holmes firmly informed Mr. Townshore that any further talk of the man in the maroon suit could wait until we arrived at the gallery. Mr. Townshore took Holmes' advice and ordered some dinner, and over the next half-hour the conversation centered around Holmes' musings on the career and legacy of his great-uncle, the French artist Vernet.

Once we'd all finished our generous servings of bread and butter pudding, we started on our walk to the gallery. Holmes peppered Mr. Townshore with a handful of additional questions regarding the details of the damage, though our new acquaintance's memory was not nearly as helpful as Holmes wished. Eventually, we reached the gallery, where three men were standing in the entryway. Mr. Townshore identified the eldest, a stocky man with a large, gleaming forehead, as Mr. Bradnick. A wispy man with a trace of cropped rusty hair was introduced to us as the artist Auguste Pilston; and a tall, strongly built fellow with a light brown mane that fell past his shoulders was the successful painter Marcus Hallard.

It took mere seconds to make the proper introductions, and the moment after Holmes mentioned that he had been asked to investigate the vandalism, Bradnick burst into a rage that made me fear that he would fall into an apoplectic fit. My remonstrations to convince him to calm himself down met with no success whatsoever.

"Calm down! Like hell I'll calm down!" Bradnick's face was now approaching the color of a beet, and he began pounding his walking stick against the floor with such vehemence that I was sure that either the cane or the tiles would crack, but I wasn't sure which would be damaged first. "This is a deliberate attack on my life and legacy! I've devoted my entire career to finding the best and most beautiful works of art that London's painters have to offer, and now, and decades of building up a reputation, I'm going to be a laughingstock! No artist is going to want his pictures to be displayed in my gallery if there's a chance that they're going to be defaced. I just know the connoisseurs are going to amble into my gallery and crack snide remarks like "This portrait's nice, but do you have any with a man in a maroon suit on them?" My business is ruined! And now that I've finally got some top-drawer talent displaying their work here…"

"Thank you so much for your kind words," Hallard replied lazily. "And you needn't worry about my continued willingness to work with you. So far, I haven't suffered in any way. My work remains unharmed."

"I wish that I could say the same," Pilston sighed. "All five of my paintings have that ridiculous little fellow prancing about in the background. They're ruined!"

Hallard laughed, but there was an unpleasant undertone. "I don't know if "ruined" is the right word to use, my dear Auguste. That would imply your little efforts had any artistic value whatsoever. I rather think that the presence of the little man has made your work much more charming, if not actually any better, really."

Pilston turned scarlet, and jerked his arm back, closing his fingers into a fist.

"None of that," Holmes said sharply, as he placed his hand over Pilston's fist. "Now is not the time for violence. Right now, if you want to do some good, I suggest that you answer all of my questions about this vandalism."

"What are you doing here?" Pilston asked. That is actually a bowdlerized version of his question. The original query was marked by a couple of profane terms that would not be accepted by my readership, so I have taken the initiative to delete them here.

"As you heard just a few seconds ago, I am Sherlock Holmes, and I am a detective. If you would be so kind as to give me a tour of this gallery and point out the damage, it would be my pleasure to assist in finding the person responsible."

Pilston quivered and looked as if he was much too furious to provide any help to Holmes, but Bradnick leapt forward, pushed Pilston to one side with a red, beefy hand, and offered his other hand to Holmes. "Sir, it's a pleasure to finally meet you. I've been following your adventures for some time, and I'd be honored if you would please condescend to use your enormous talents on this little problem. I know it's not a murder or a bank robbery or an affair of state– I'm afraid you might see this as something of no more interest than a nasty little scribbling on a public lavatory wall– but to me, this gallery is hallowed ground to me. You must excuse my tantrum a moment ago. I have a notoriously short fuse. Always have, and probably always will. Your name didn't sink in for a while, but when I finally realized who you were right now, I thanked my lucky stars, because you're just the man I need to figure out who performed this little joke."

Holmes smiled. "Thank you, sir. I'm glad to see that you have calmed down and are approaching this matter in a much more constructive way."

Hallard laughed again. I did not like his laugh at all. It sounded as if it came from a man who treated the rest of humanity with contempt, and his eyes were cold and joyless. "I didn't want to point out that you were indulging in an awful tizzy of hyperbole a few minutes ago, but if you'd only take a moment to observe exactly which picture sere damaged, you'd realize that there's nothing very much to get upset over, is there? After all, it's only the cheap pictures that are damaged. The valuable art– the work by talented fellows like myself, that's all untouched. None of it is damaged in the slightest. But the dreck– the work by the artists you only give a place as a favor in order to give them a chance at finding an audience for their tawdry little attempts at creation, those are the pictures where the maroon man has made his appearances. Grissold's appalling landscapes. Frug's lifeless panormas. And Pilston's... Well, I'm not sure what word you'd apply to his wastes of perfectly good paint, other than "garbage.""

Pilston swore again and lunged at Hallard, who seemed highly amused by the attack. Hallard performed a little backwards shuffle and pivoted on his left heel, and Pilston couldn't correct his balance in time, so he fell forward in a painful-looking somersault. I stepped forward in an attempt to perform my duties as a medical professional, but before I could examine Pilston, he waved me away, raised himself up, whipped out his handkerchief, and began wiping away dust that was invisible to my eyes, muttering vulgarities under his breath all the while.

Holmes observed Pilston with a look that might have been a glare of contempt or a gaze of repressed amusement. I could not tell which. Once Pilston had dusted off his entire body, Holmes took a deep breath and asked Bradnick, "Sir, would you like me to investigate the damage to the pictures in your gallery?"

Bradnick was not the sort of man to limit himself to two words when he had the ability to use hundreds, and after a few minutes of ranting and politely yet loudly asking for Holmes' help, Holmes finally cut him off and announced his acceptance of the case. "I should like to interview each of you shortly, but for the moment I shall need to examine the entire gallery. I trust that you can all be reasonably quiet long enough for me to concentrate and make the necessary observations?"

Pilston pocketed his handkerchief in a failed attempt to appear dignified. "Mr. Holmes, I shall be delighted to help you, but I shall not stand around in silence, wasting my time. I believe that I shall go out and purchase an evening newspaper. I'll return shortly."

Hallard made a half-hearted attempt to suppress a yawn. "I am rather peckish. There'a baked-potato cart down the street. Would anybody else care for one?" As there were no takers, Hallard shrugged and ambled out the door.

Bradnick's face was still unnaturally mottled. "I'll be going to my office and pouring myself a very stiff drink." As he walked away, Holmes withdrew his powerful magnifying lens from his coat pocket and began a circuit of the gallery, examining each portrait in turn, whether or not it had a little man in a maroon suit in it, though he paid particularly close attention to each image of the unusually-dressed man. I followed Holmes around, and though I possessed no item to aid in my examination, I scrutinized each picture to the best of my ability. Luckily, Townshore's estimates were high, and there were only one hundred forty-two pictures in the gallery, and just fifty-one of them had the maroon-suited man added to them.

Our examination of the gallery lasted just under an hour, though none of the three men who had left had returned yet. Townshore had perched himself on a windowsill near the entryway, and had spent the entire time nibbling away at his fingernails. Holmes didn't seem to be in any hurry to speak to the other gentlemen. After looking over the last painting, which featured the maroon suit man performing what appeared to be an awkward soft shoe dance, Holmes leaned against the wall and started tapping his

49

magnifying lens against his palm, as he stared up at the ceiling. I stood there quietly and watched the gears of his mind turn for a while. After several minutes, I regret to say that my impatience got the better of me, and I interrupted Holmes' reverie to prompt him to share his thoughts.

"I was thinking… about fairy tales."

His answer stupefied me. The thought of Holmes reflecting on Cinderella and Sleeping Beauty seemed painfully out of character. My friend noticed my amazement, and with no shortage of amusement in his face, elaborated on his comment.

"Are you familiar with the story of Ali Baba and the Forty Thieves from the Arabian Nights? Or Hans Christian Andersen's The Tinder Box?"

"I'm fairly sure that I read them as a child, but adulthood has wiped them from my memory."

"Both of them contain the same plot point. In Ali Baba and the Forty Thieves, a clever family servant notices that someone has marked the door of their house with a piece of chalk, so she takes some chalk and places an identical mark on every other front door on the street. In the Tinder Box, a dog with enormous eyes performs exactly the same trick to save his master."

"And what do clever servants and big-eyed dogs have to do with this defaced gallery, Holmes?"

"My dear fellow, consider this possibility. Only one of these little men in maroon serves a purpose. The others are merely decoys."

"I don't follow you."

"Have you noticed what all of the vandalized pictures have in common, Watson? Aside from the nature of the addition, what quality connects the paintings that had the maroon man added, and which were left undamaged?"

I reflected for a moment. "Only the oil paintings had the little maroon man added. None of the watercolors were altered."

"True. But there are only thirteen watercolors in the gallery. All the rest are oils, and there are many oil paintings that were not harmed."

I thought for a little while, trying to find a link in the subject matters. Eventually, I conceded defeat.

"You're focusing on the pictures themselves, Watson. Look at the little cards tacked to the side of each picture."

I took a quick walk around the gallery, and midway through my review, I realized something notable. "Only the cheapest pictures have been vandalized!"

Holmes chuckled. "Precisely, my dear fellow. All of the damaged pictures have been created by the same seven artists, and—" He lowered his voice so that Mr. Townshore couldn't hear him. "They are the least talented of the artists displayed at the gallery. None of their pictures are priced at more than twenty pounds, and most of them are worth even less. And none of these works are likely to rise in value, either. Of course, I do not profess to be an expert in art, but I feel fairly confident that the artistic merit of the damaged paintings is of fairly low quality. In contrast, the paintings that remained untouched are being valued at minimum, a hundred pounds apiece, and many of them are fetching a price of several times that. The creators of those paintings are, to my untrained eye, far more worthy of the higher price than their more amateurish peers. About a dozen of them are quite valuable. Those have real historical value, and are worth well over a thousand pounds.

"Do you think that the vandal was afraid he'd get caught, and didn't want to get billed for damaging the priciest works?"

"I think that the motive has a touch more nobility than that, Watson. Consider this. The vandal didn't want to damage a work of genuine art. He couldn't bear to deface something created by someone with genuine talent."

"You're being as clear as mulligatawny soup, Holmes."

"Let's take a look at some of Hallard's paintings. Whatever personality defects the fellow may have, even his harshest critics can concede that he can paint. There's genuine warmth in those portraits, they have a real glow that makes them seem almost lifelike. No hack can create that sort of effect. It takes true talent. The pictures are fetching prices from five to seven hundred pounds apiece, and though I would never pay that much myself, even if I had that kind of money to fritter away, I still concede that the gallery is justified in asking such a price."

"I'd disagree, but I don't want to start an argument."

"That's very generous of you, Watson. Now, take a good look at the pictures created by Pilston. What do you think of them?"

I leaned forward and examined the price. "This picture of a picnic is going for fifteen pounds. I wouldn't give five for it." I paused, then added, "I'm really not sure if that little man in maroon actually adds to the painting or damages it." The maroon man was sitting next to a lady in a blue dress, eating a sandwich.

"Indeed, Watson. Compare the man in the maroon suit to the others at the picnic. Does anything strike your eye?"

I pondered for a while, and then surrendered. "Sorry, Holmes. I'm coming up empty here."

My friend looked regretful. "We'll leave it there for a bit, then. Take a look at this other picture by Pilston. This one, with three deer in a field."

I shrugged. "Twenty pounds. Still overpriced, but I do like it much more than the picnic one." The maroon suit man was petting the largest of the deer.

"What is your critique of the artwork?"

"Nothing special, I'd say."

"I would be the first to note that much of the painting– the grass, the shrubs, the clouds in the sky… all of those are fairly pedestrian. Clumsy work, really. But observe the eyes of the deer, Watson. Don't you see the spark of life in them? And that little tree off to the right. Do you see the skill that went into that to give it a three-dimensional effect?"

After Holmes pointed it out, I could see it. "But what does that mean?"

"It means that Pilston's work is rather like that cartoon in *Punch* about the curate's egg– parts of it are excellent! Mr. Pilston does have a flair for painting, but for the lion's share of the picture, he is willing to content himself with producing flat and uninspired work."

"A bit harsh, Holmes."

"Not so, Watson, just stating a fact. Mr. Pilston has talent, yet he chooses to paint pictures as if he's a first-year student at a disreputable art school. These are pictures painted by a man who isn't putting very much effort into his compositions."

I thought for a few moments of my time as a schoolboy, and how one of the more brilliant fellows of my acquaintance consistently scored just enough points on his exams to pass, even though he could have earned a place at the top of the class if he had only tried. When I'd asked him about his marks not reflecting his potential, he'd laughingly explained that school was boring, as the eldest son of a prominent peer of the realm his future was assured even if he was illiterate. He proclaimed that his time would be far better spent exploring topics of real interest to him, although he never explained to me what he considered more intriguing than school. Upon further reflection, the comparison didn't appear to be a particularly apt one, since my classmate was a privileged young man, and Pilston was a man who was probably trying to make a living off his art, so it would be in his interest to create the best pictures possible.

I voiced my thoughts to Holmes, who smiled and replied, "Quite right, Watson. Now, how would you judge the images of the man in the maroon suit?"

"On an artistic level? Nothing very notable. A bit crude, rather more of a cartoon than a realistic representation of a person."

"True, the artwork is rough, but notice the form and style of the brushwork. Though unrefined, it shows a familiarity with human anatomy, not like the completely untrained, who reduce the form of the body to a compilation of shapeless blobs."

"The artist was probably in a rush."

"I concede your point, but the argument I am advancing is the fact that no matter how much a skilled artist tries to hide his talent, he can never truly produce work at the same level as a rank amateur. So now we have two collections of works that reflect suppressed talent. I cannot expect you to draw the same conclusions I did, due to the fact that you lacked a magnifying lens of your own, but after a careful examination of the brushstroke patterns used to create the maroon suit man and Pilston's paintings, I would wager my violin that they were created by the same man."

"Pilston is the vandal? But why would he damage his own paintings?"

"From the lack of effort he put into them, it's obvious that he doesn't care about them very much."

"But Holmes, what would be the purpose of this entire charade?"

"The answer comes from observing everything, old chap. You thought that I was only examining the pictures, didn't you? You really ought to have known better my friend. You know my methods. I examined the walls and floor as well and found..." Here Holmes crossed the room and pointed at a pair of small dark ovals on the wainscoting. "These."

I scrutinized them. "I can't be certain without that test of yours, but could they be blood?"

"I'm fairly certain of that. There are other, tinier droplets here–" he pointed. "And there. And there. Given the lighting, they're easy to miss."

"But what does this mean? Was someone injured?"

"One can only hope it was something so simple and comparatively harmless." Holmes's mouth twitched upward into a wry smile. "I dare say that if you choose to write an account of this adventure, the odds of your recording my covering myself in glory are far outweighed by the probability that in less than a minute, I shall humiliate myself so badly that I shall have no choice but to abandon detecting forever and take up bee-farming in the countryside."

"Heaven forbid, Holmes. But what are you thinking?"

"Watson, the droplets on the wall suggest that some unfortunate person was killed here. From the angle and shape of the blood, I would suspect a stabbing. It's my belief that after the murder, some blood spattered on one of the paintings, most likely this one here. Now, after the killer hid the body and wiped away as much of the blood as he could find, he came back and realized that he had to cover up the bloodstain on the picture. He couldn't wash it off the oil paint, so he came up with the idea to cover it with something– a man in a maroon suit. The problem was, the image would draw a great deal of attention, so the killer realized that the best way to disguise his vandalism would be to paint similar figures on as many other painting as he could."

"This "he" you refer to, are you referring to Pilston?"

"I am. If you observed, his jacket pocket contained a little case, the kind artists use to carry brushes and some tubes of oils, so we know he would have paint handy."

"But who did he kill? And why?"

"You'll notice that he only damaged the cheap, poorer quality paintings. When I scrutinized the pictures, I discovered that several paintings, the older ones costing over a thousand pounds, had brush strokes that matched some of Pilston's paintings."

"Forgery? Pilston replaced the valuable paintings with his own copies?"

"Precisely. And his victim walked in on him in the act, and the poor woman died simply because she was in the wrong place at the wrong time."

"Who is this woman?"

"The charwoman, of course. Pilston came in during the night to make his latest switch, she saw what she was doing, and he stabbed her with his pocketknife. You can tell that the gallery hasn't been cleaned in a few days. The rest of the coverup occurred as I said."

"What did he do with the body?"

"I can't say for certain before further examination. He must have found a hiding place nearby, hid the unfortunate lady, and I suspect he's spent most of the past hour trying to move the corpse. In any case, Townshore hasn't left that windowsill, I can hear Bradnick and the sound of clinking glass in his office, and you can see Hallard sitting on the wall out that window there, munching on a baked potato and reading a newspaper. As far as I can tell, Pilston is nowhere to be found–"

Holmes' voice faded away as a couple of police officers appeared in the window, with a handcuffed Pilston in tow. Holmes let them inside, greeted them, and asked, "I presume you caught Mr. Pilston attempting to dispose of a woman's body?"

One policeman's eyes widened. "Yes. How did you know?"

Holmes summarized his conclusions, and surprisingly, Pilston chimed in every few moments to confirm what Holmes had deduced. If being amazingly right based on scanty evidence was feeding his ego, he did a remarkable job of disguising his self-satisfaction. Pilston, for his part, was being a remarkably good sport about his capture, and he accepted his fate with more grace than I'd ever seen before or since.

"Just one more question," Holmes asked Pilston as the police led the criminal away. "Why on earth did you choose to paint that little man in a maroon suit?"

Pilston shrugged his shoulders. "I had a limited amount of paint with me, and not many colors. I just so happened to have a lot of maroon paint, so it seemed like a sensible idea at the time to make that the color of the man's suit."

Merridew of Abominable Memory

"My collection of M's is a fine one," said he. "Moriarty himself is enough to make any letter illustrious, and here is Morgan the poisoner, and Merridew of abominable memory, and Mathews, who knocked out my left canine in the waiting-room at Charing Cross, and, finally, here is our friend of to-night."

–"The Empty House"

"Thank heavens you're back, Doctor. I'm at my wits' end trying to figure out what to do next."

My landlady, Mrs. Hudson, was rarely flustered, but this evening, she seemed terribly shaken.

"What on earth is the matter?"

"Well, you've been gone for three days visiting your army friend, Doctor, and Mr. Holmes has been away for even longer, working on another of his cases. But the night after you left, this gentleman knocked on the door and insisted on coming inside. Well, I tried to tell him I didn't know when Mr. Holmes would be back. It might be a few minutes, or it might be a few days. He didn't care. He said he had no idea who this Mr. Holmes was, but I could show him in when he arrived. He was adamant on waiting in your rooms, even though I said that I didn't like leaving a stranger there with both of you away. But I couldn't stop him, Doctor, he just staggered up the stairs, sat down in a chair, and said that he needed rest and wouldn't listen to a word I said, and to the best of my knowledge, he hasn't stirred from that chair."

"Not for nearly three days?"

"Well, if he's gotten up to stretch his legs or answer a call of nature I haven't heard him. I've been checking in on him every hour, and he's starting to gather dust, he is. Mind you, I'm not in the habit of doling out free meals to strangers who show up at the doorstep, but I don't think he's eaten a crumb since he arrived. Do you know what he said when I asked him if he'd had his dinner?"

"What?"

"He said, "Dinner? What's that?" And then he turned his head to one side and started staring at the window. Only the curtains were drawn, Doctor. That's a very odd duck, if I do say so myself. I think you'd better see what he wants, hadn't you?"

"Absolutely! Did you give you his name or tell you why he came here?"

"I asked him, Doctor, and I tell you, his answer made the hairs on the back of my neck stand on end. Shall I tell you what he said?"

"Yes! Please don't keep me in suspense!"

"Very well. He told me, "I don't know. Don't ask me again." And then he closed his eyes and wouldn't say another word, not even when I spoke directly into his ear."

I was dumbstruck. "Are you saying he claims not to be able to recall his own *name*?"

"Exactly. I thought he was having a joke at my expense at first, but when I looked at him closely, I didn't see the faintest hint of a smile. It makes no sense to say this, but I think he meant it."

"But that's absurd."

"With all due respect, Doctor, you should be telling him that, not me."

I saw the justice in this comment, and I hurried up to my rooms and opened the door. I saw no one at first, until I approached the fireplace and discovered a small, elderly man sitting in one of the high-backed chairs.

He didn't appear to notice me at first, until I cleared my throat and his body quivered and he finally looked up to meet my chilly gaze. "Who are you and what do you want?" he demanded.

It took a bit of effort, but I managed to keep the asperity I was feeling out of my voice. "My name is Dr. John Watson and this is my home. May I ask who you are and what you are doing here?"

My guest did not seem upset or surprised by my reply. "Are you sure?"

"Of course I am. I know for certain who I am and where I live. Can you say the same?"

He clenched his jaw. "This is my home." He paused. "I think it is." His voice quavered and cracked. "I thought it was."

My annoyance vanished as I suddenly realized that this man might be suffering from some sort of stroke or dementia. "Sir, I am a medical doctor, and I think I should examine you to see if you are–"

"No!" His voice grew so loud and shrill that I felt my eardrums vibrate. "I won't be touched! You can't! You have no right! This is my house! Leave me alone!"

Involuntarily, I took a couple of steps back, but regained my composure when the suddenly enraged man shook and deflated like a punctured balloon, until he was just a frightened and lost-looking old fellow.

I approached him again. "Sir, what is your name?"

He looked agonized. "My name? Don't you know?"

"I do not, sir. I'm afraid we're strangers."

"How bizarre. I wonder what you're doing here, then."

"Sir, what is your name?"

"I… I think I know. I ought to know it. I just need time to think of it. Give me time. Give me time!" He clasped his head in his hands and rocked back in forth in the chair. I placed my hand on his shoulder in an attempt to steady him, but he slapped my arm away immediately. He was quite frail, so he caused me no pain by striking me, and my overarching emotions were of concern for him rather than annoyance.

The next two hours followed the same pattern. I would attempt to examine him, he would fight me off, I would ask his name, he would be unable to answer, then he would ask me my name and demand to know what I was doing in his home. When I would patiently re-introduce and re-re-introduce myself, he would become disoriented and confused. All attempts to come close to him were rebuffed, and I was starting to grow frustrated when the door swung open and Holmes made his welcome return.

After greeting him and quickly apprising him of the situation, the familiar interest glint entered Holmes' eye, and he strode over to the fireplace without even taking off his coat. "Good evening, sir. My name is Sherlock Holmes."

"Who?"

Holmes was compelled to repeat his name thrice, each time receiving the same response, until he finally asked for our guest's name, and received a response similar to the ones our guest gave me.

Looking thoughtful, Holmes rang for Mrs. Hudson. When she arrived, he asked for tea and scones. When they arrived, he filled a cup and handed it to our anonymous visitor. "Your tea, sir."

"My… tea?"

"That is correct. I suggest that you drink it while it is hot."

Obediently, our guest took the cup and sipped. When its contents were nearly emptied, he started sagging, and the cup tilted and began to slip from his fingers. Holmes snatched the cup from him before the dregs spilled, and chuckled as he sank his teeth into a scone.

"Holmes, what did you put into that tea?"

"A bit of sugar. It disguises the taste of the mild narcotic I slipped into the cup."

"But you can't just go about knocking out people with drugs!"

"This is a special circumstance, Watson. Our guest is clearly ill and will not allow us to examine him. This is the most efficient and humane way to subdue him." Scrutinizing our visitor as he slipped into unconsciousness, Holmes took a sip from a teacup that I presumed was devoid of narcotics. "I think he'll be more amenable to an examination now. I suggest that you start immediately. The dose I gave him was so tiny that I doubt that he'll need more than fifteen minutes or so before awakening."

Setting my last, lingering concerns about medical ethics aside, I started to look over our guest. He was not in the best health. The fact that he quite likely had not consumed any nutrients or water in the last few days aside from his recent cup of tea had left him weak and dehydrated. Yet it was clear that he had been in decline for some months previously, and from the pallor on his skin and a handful of other indicators, I suspected that he was in the advanced stages of some sort of cancer.

I voiced my initial diagnosis to Holmes, who was in the middle of his second scone. "Could his disorientation be due to a brain tumor?"

"Anything is possible. I need to examine him more closely. It's possible that a stroke or an aneurism, or simply senility, caused this."

"Or a blow to the head?"

"That's possible, yes." Our guest's head was largely bald, but as I examined the eggshell-colored fringe along the edges of his skull, I noticed a little brown patch the size of the nail on my littlest finger. "Holmes! Look at this!" I pointed to a small piece of metal that was sticking out of the back of his head. "What is that? Could it be a nail?"

"There's no head to it, and the edge is rough, like it was snapped off... An ice pick, perhaps?" Holmes picked up his magnifying glass, nodded in response to my warning not to touch the metal projection, studied the wound, and handed the magnifying glass to me. After examining it, I returned the magnifying glass to Holmes and informed him, "I would say that this man was stabbed in the head, most likely with an ice pick. The wound almost certainly caused lasting brain damage and probably permanently impaired his memory."

"Abominable. Is it possible to remove the weapon to study it?"

"At this point, I would strongly advise against it. To pull out the weapon might cause even more damage, and would possibly even kill the patient. Perhaps a skilled surgeon specializing in brain disorders might be able to operate, but to attempt to do anything with the wound here would be so foolhardy that any doctor who attempted to perform such a procedure might justifiably be expelled from the profession."

Holmes shook his head. "That is unfortunate on multiple levels. Yet now that you know the cause of this man's memory impairment, you can say with certainty that he requires proper medical attention?"

"Of course! Not only for his wound, but for his malnutrition, dehydration, and general illness as well."

With a nod, Holmes crossed the room and summoned our page-boy. When he arrived moments later, Holmes told him, "Go and fetch an ambulance at once. Inform them that we have a gravely ill and wounded man here, and he requires urgent medical attention. Quickly now."

As the lad sprinted away, I shook my head. "It's amazing that the man was able to walk and retain so many of his cognitive functions after suffering such a terrible wound, but such things do happen. Though in his condition, I'm not sure whether to dub him lucky or not."

"Where there's life, there's hope, Watson, and in any case, we have to make use of the precious time we have before the ambulance arrives and takes away our guest." Holmes immediately started searching the pockets of the unconscious man. I started to make some sort of objection, but Holmes waved a dismissive hand at me. "If we are to find out who attacked this man, we will need all the information we can obtain, and first on the list is the man's name."

After completing his preliminary search, Holmes sighed. "No wallet. The man was the victim of a pickpocket."

"Surely he could have simply misplaced his wallet or left it behind. We don't know how or where he received his injury."

"First of all, Watson, I will draw your attention to these greasy smears and coal-dust on the inside of this poor man's pocket where most men keep their wallets. This man's hands have not been washed recently, but they are not nearly at that level of uncleanliness and are well-manicured. Obviously, another hand, not his own, dipped into his pocket and extracted his wallet. No doubt some filthy denizen of the streets saw our visitor in his discombobulated state and thought he was a wealthy and easy mark, so he picked his pocket."

"He? There are female pickpockets you know, Holmes."

"If you were to look at the size of the dirty smears in that pocket, Watson, you would know it was unlikely that a woman's hand could have created that level of damage. We also know that he was attacked at night, inside a building where he felt comfortable and safe and where he was prepared to spend a substantial period of time, though not, most likely, his own home."

I was still smarting from Holmes' rebuttal to my female pickpocket remark, so I said nothing, and Holmes, looking disappointed at my missing my cue, continued. "You'll note that our guest is clad in evening wear, Watson. Quite expensive, well-tailored, surely, this fellow is a man of means. But he has no coat, no hat, and no scarf. That is because he removed those garments upon entering the domicile he visited when he was attacked. He was probably not in his own home because had he let himself in with his own key, which he would have then returned to his pocket, the key would have been at the top of the pocket's contents. Instead, this handkerchief rests on top of the key, suggesting that he has had need of it since he last used his key. His hands, though not dirty enough to cause the smears in his pockets, still have evident traces of street grime on them, but no corresponding marks are on his handkerchief, indicating that he has not used it in some time. Furthermore, the man clearly suffers from corns and chilblains on his feet, and his shoes look to be a fraction too tight for him. Unless a man is expecting company, if his dress shoes cause him discomfort, he will remove them upon reaching his own house. He has transferred his wedding ring from his left to his right hand, indicating that he is a widower. Given the care with which this button was resewn to his cuff, I think it likely that he keeps a manservant. Now coming back to the handkerchief…"

Holmes unfolded the square of white cloth in front of me with a dramatic flourish. "It bears the initials "T.M." Clearly our guest's initials. His pocket watch…" Holmes pressed the latch and opened it. "Contains a telling inscription. To Thaddeus, a wonderful husband and father on our 25th anniversary. Love, your darling Jewel." Jewel is clearly his late wife, and our man is Thaddeus M. We must track down this man's child or children, Watson. If he has been here for three days, they might be aware of his absence and worried."

"Is there nothing else you can deduce, Holmes?"

My friend looked the unconscious man up and down a few times, before uttering a quick exclamation of triumph. "Observe, Watson! A foreign hair clinging to his own hair. White horsehair that has yellowed. From its length and the curls on it, it comes from a judge's wig! Watson, examine our copy of *Who's Who*, go to the M's, and see if you can find a judge named Thaddeus with a wife named Jewel, though upon further reflection, "Jewel" may be pet name for his wife."

I obeyed and began scanning pages while Holmes applied his standard level of scrutiny to T.M.'s hands and feet. A few minutes passed, until I finally found an entry that met our specifications. "This could be him, Holmes! Thaddeus Merridew. High Court Judge, his wife Jillian passed away two years ago."

""Jewel" might feasibly be a sobriquet for "Jill," Holmes noted. "The usual information on his residence is present?"

"Yes. 2218 Guilders Lane. Not much more information, other than a couple of clubs and the fact that he has a son currently working in Belfast and a married daughter living in India."

"Then we have a solid thread to follow," Holmes replied. "I could not find much more of use on his extremities, save for the fact that he was in the habit of carrying a silver-headed walking stick that he needed for a limp in his left leg."

Why fight it? I asked myself. "And how did you deduce that, Holmes?"

"The scuffing on his left shoe indicates a limp. When a cane is carried to alleviate leg pain or damage, it is generally held in the opposite hand from the afflicted leg. On his right hand, I found traces of silver polish. Clearly, he lost his walking stick soon after the attack. As the cane was not merely decorative, he would not have left it at the door along with his coat and hat."

A knock at the door showed us that the ambulance had arrived, and the presumed Mr. Merridew, who was just starting to emerge from his stupor, was eased onto a stretcher and carried away to the hospital. At Holmes' suggestion, I continued making my way through the "M's" just in case there was a second potential name that fit our profile. There was none, and so, once the remaining scones and tea were consumed, we left to investigate.

A knock at the door of Justice Merridew's home brought a ruffled-looking valet to the door. After explaining that his master was not at home, Holmes informed him that we were aware of the fact that his employer had been missing for the last few days and that the judge had been found and was now in the hospital. Our request to be allowed in to ask some questions was accepted. As we entered, Holmes tapped the address plate on the pillar by the door.

"This may explain why Justice Merridew came to our residence and had the fixed impression that it was his house, Watson. He had been wandering the streets of London for some time before he reached our room, probably for the better part of a day, given the very slight about of the dust and dirt of the city on his clothes, and the fact that he was not at death's door from dehydration. His brain was damaged, and what remained of his mental faculties was devoted to finding something, anything with a semblance of familiarity to his home. When he saw our address plate for 221B, he misread it for his own 2218, and in his impaired mental state he became convinced that he had reached his own dwelling."

Since he was to talk to us, the valet was clearly uncertain as to whether he should allow us into the main sitting room, where the judge's guests were welcomed, or if he should lead us into the small back room where he was allowed to meet with his own acquaintances. Holmes, no doubt correctly deducing that the chairs would be far more comfortable in the judge's siting room, settled into a plush chair, and I followed suit.

"Your name, please?" Holmes asked after introducing ourselves.

"Tenners, sir."

"How long have you been working for Justice Merridew?"

"Just over four years, sir. I started working for him right after Mrs. Merridew fell ill with her long ailment."

"When was the last time you saw him?"

"Just a few days ago, sir. He had a dinner engagement at The Golden Nectarine, and I prepared his clothes and polished the silver handle his walking stick."

"Can you describe the clothing and cane?"

"An ordinary long black dinner dress coat, a white scarf, and a black top hat. Exactly the same garments worn by thousands of other gentlemen, sir. The walking stick had a handle shaped like a lion's head."

"Do you know who the judge was going to meet for dinner?"

"I do not, sir. My employer is not in the habit of providing me with any details besides what I absolutely need to know for my duties. I was told to expect him back by midnight. I was waiting up until three for him, sir. When he didn't arrive I made some discreet enquiries, but I was waiting to inform the police out of fear of a scandal. The judge would not have liked that at all, sir. He was most reluctant to cross paths with the police unless it was absolutely necessary. He considered it ungentlemanly."

"You ought to have come to me," Holmes replied.

"You were away investigating a case until an hour ago, with no information on how to find you," I reminded him.

"True enough," my friend conceded. "Do you have any knowledge as to anyone who might want to do the judge harm?"

"None, sir," Tenners answered. "He had no enemies that I know of, but perhaps someone at the Old Bailey might have had a better idea. I dare say a magistrate upsets a lot of people with his rulings, but he never shared any details with me."

"No angry or threatening letters?"

"I don't open his mail, sir. I just gather it. He keeps his recent correspondence on that salver there, if you'd care to look."

Holmes examined the stack of envelopes, and found nothing of note. Thanking Tenners for his time, we took a hansom to The Golden Nectarine, where we were told that Merridew had a reservation for two that night, but he had never arrived. Another man named Ivers had arrived and asked for Merridew, but after an hour passed with no sign of the judge, Ivers had left. Having learned almost nothing of use, we travelled to the Old Bailey to investigate at the judge's chambers.

On our way, we passed two men, a young fellow in his early twenties, and a distinguished-looking mad in his mid-sixties wearing a barrister's robe. We would not have given them a second look had we not heard the younger man refer to the elder as "Mr. Ivers." It took only a few moments to introduce ourselves and explain our purpose. Ivers expressed concern and stated that he was happy to do whatever he could to assist us, and his young friend murmured a polite goodbye and slipped away.

"I suspected that something was terribly wrong," Ivers declared. "Thaddeus is never late and he would never miss an appointment. I was certain that *I* had made a mistake of the date, but I was informed at the restaurant that Thaddeus had reserved a table. I was quite certain that something had happened, but I was not sure what to do– I didn't have his home address handy, and when I didn't see him around here the last few days, I had a word with his clerk, although he's an elderly fellow and prone to letting things slip his mind. Thaddeus should have forced him into retirement years ago, but they've worked together for most of their professional lives, though Thaddeus has kept his mind sharp as a tack."

Holmes shook his head. "Unfortunately, his mental powers have probably been forever destroyed by the attack." Ivers asked for details, and the lawyer grew horrified as he learned of the damage to his friend's mind.

"Good heavens! How distressing!" Ivers patted his face with a handkerchief. "Is there any hope of a recovery?"

"Unlikely," I said. "In any case, given his overall bad health… I don't know if you were aware…"

Ivers nodded. "He was diagnosed with cancer about seven months ago. They said it would be unlikely that he would make it to Christmas. Poor fellow. We'd often talked about what we'd do

78

during our retirements. Thaddeus thought of moving to a warmer climate. And now… Would you happen to know which hospital they took him to? I should like to visit him."

I provided him with the requested information, and Ivers nodded and excused himself, noting that he had to meet with a client. As he walked away from us, Holmes called out to him, "By the way, Mr. Ivers. Did you never think of talking to the police about your missing friend?"

Ivers looked horrified. "Of course not. A gentleman never has anything to do with police if he can help it."

Once Ivers turned around the corner and out of sight, Holmes murmured to me, "He's lying, of course."

"Whatever makes you say that, Holmes?"

"A man like that doesn't just assume that his missing terminally ill friend will be all right and does nothing, no matter how much he dislikes the police. No, there's more to it than that. He's hiding something important, and I rather suspect that he's bribed the valet Tenners as well."

"Do you have a reason for those suspicions?"

"Tenners was nervous, and clearly had something weighing on his conscience. My guess is that Ivers wanted to keep Tenners from raising the alarm. Perhaps he made a threat, or more likely, suggested that it was not in Tenners' interests to create a potential scandal, and slipped him a little money to assuage his conscience."

"Do you really think that Ivers harmed his friend?"

"No," Holmes frowned. "I don't. First of all, Ivers is not the sort of man who allows his own hands to get dirty, especially not with blood. I have a feeling that there's a significant link or two or three in the chain that we're missing." He paused and looked reflective. "Watson, do you remember the positioning of the wound? The direction of the thrust of the ice pick?"

I needed a moment to search my memory. "The bit of metal was pointing downwards, wasn't it?"

"It was. And Merridew was a small man. The stab came from an upwards direction. Which means that either his assailant was diminutive, or…"

At first I thought that Holmes was pausing for dramatic effect, but after time passed with no continuation, I realized that my friend was concentrating. After a few people stared at Holmes for acting like a statue, I gave him a little nudge, prompting him to say, "What I can't understand is, why didn't the assailant follow Merridew to finish the job? Why didn't he strike again with another weapon, or why not restrain him somehow? After all, the odds were likely that his erratic behavior would catch the attention of a police officer. Surely the villain could have caught up with an elderly, injured, seriously ill man. Unless..." Thankfully, Holmes didn't try my patience with too long a pause. "Watson! I've got it! The assailant was in a wheelchair!"

I begged him for some explanation.

"It makes perfect sense. Why didn't Merridew's attacker follow him out the door and try to kill him again? Because he couldn't, Watson! Whoever did this was too weak in the legs to go after him, though the would-be killer was strong enough to stab him with an ice pick. We must go back to The Golden Nectarine immediately and search the neighborhood."

"For what, Holmes?"

"For a ramp, Watson! A private home with an entrance designed for someone in a wheelchair!"

As we began the journey back to The Golden Nectarine, I informed Holmes that I thought that he was making a logical leap here, and I was surprised to see that he agreed with me. "Indeed, Watson, I may be going beyond the limits of pure logic here. I could be putting two and two together and making five, or even five million. If I get egg on my face, you have my permission to record my humiliation with total accuracy in one of your literary endeavors. In the meantime, let us see what my deductive leaps produce."

We spent twenty minutes walking around the neighborhood surrounding The Golden Nectarine in a spiral, until Holmes yelped in triumph. "A ramp, Watson! This house has a ramp!"

He noticed the ramp from about twenty yards away. As I struggled to keep up with him, I reminded him that there are many people in London in wheelchairs. "I am well aware of that, Watson," he replied, "but if this does not prove to be the domicile in question, then we shall simply have to look elsewhere. If we have beaten the odds and this is indeed the spot we're searching for, then a young, pretty woman wearing rather too much inexpensive makeup will answer the door for us."

I was too intrigued not to ask, "How on earth did you deduce that, Holmes?"

"Did you not notice the mark on Ivers' neck, Watson? Cheap rouge, the kind a young woman of modest background will slather on in an attempt to get the attention she desires. Ivers has a wedding ring, and in any event, a barrister of that standing will have been prudent in his selection of a wife in his youth, but rather more reckless in his selection of a mistress in his later years. A respectable barrister's wife would not coat herself with that sort of cosmetic, nor would Ivers approve of his daughter adorning herself in such a manner." Having reached the house, Holmes immediately bent over the hand rail at the side of the ramp and began to sniff it. "Aha! Silver polish, Watson, a faint but noticeable lingering aroma. This rail is base metal, the only reason for silver polish being there is if poor Merridew gripped it on his way out, having dropped his recently polished cane after the attack."

"Sir? What are you doing?" The front door opened, and a pretty young woman appeared in the entryway. She was tall, with long honey-colored hair and her face was indeed liberally coated with rouge, though I lacked the experience with makeup to tell the cost of this coloring.

Holmes drew himself up with remarkable dignity and replied, "I am here to speak to you, Miss, about your friendship with Mr. Ivers, as well as his friend Justice Merridew."

Even under all of that rouge, it was obvious that the girl had blanched at Ivers' name, though curiously the name of Merridew did not appear to affect her. Indeed, after displaying clear confusion for a few moments, she replied, with palpable honesty, "I've never met a Justice Merridew."

"But you *do* know a Mr. Ivers, the barrister," Holmes pounced. "Come, come. There is no point in denying it. You were seen together."

The girl looked troubled. "What do you want from me?"

"Only the truth, young lady, nothing more. And I think that if you would be so kind as to let us inside, and allow us to speak to the resident of this house who uses a wheelchair, we might be able to clear up this entire unfortunate situation."

The girl seemed hesitant to budge, though I cannot say that I blamed her. My friend was playing an excellent bluff, but if she called it, he would be unable to produce any solid evidence to support his theories, nor would he be able to even identify her by her name.

Fortunately, a reedy voice called out from behind her. "Let them in, Millicent. There's no point in dragging this out much longer."

The girl we now knew as Millicent silently stepped backwards and gestured for us to enter. It was not a luxurious or even well-maintained home, but it was obviously a place of modest comfort. Millicent led us into a small parlor, where a woman sat in one corner in a wheelchair, sipping a lemon squash. This woman could not have been too much older than fifty, but she was clearly in declining health, and if my initial impressions were correct, she was not long for this world. "Cancer," she replied, reading my mind. "It started in my throat and spread throughout my entire body. The doctors give me one to two months. I think that's generous." She sipped her lemon squash. "You're Sherlock Holmes and Dr. Watson. I've seen your pictures in the newspaper. Did the judge's family hire you to find out what happened to him?"

"No, he showed up at my home himself."

"Is he all right?"

"No, he is not. His memory has been utterly destroyed."

"So he didn't accuse me?"

"He could not. He was unaware of his own condition."

"Meaning both the wound I inflicted on him and the cancer?"

"That is correct. You're confessing to stabbing him with the ice pick, then?"

"I might as well. I'll never see the hangman's rope, though perhaps it would be less painful than this. In a way, I might have done him a favor by sparing him some of the knowledge of his own ailment."

"I am not certain that he would see it that way," Holmes replied with evident disapproval.

"No, he probably wouldn't." The woman took another sip of lemon squash. "My doctor tells me to keep drinking this. It's supposed to soothe my burning throat. It does help, but only if it's nice and cold, so I have to keep adding little chips of ice to it. That's why I had the pick handy a few nights ago. Millicent provides me with a small lump of ice, and I keep breaking off little chunks to put in my drink. Or I did, before I broke the implement." She looked at Holmes searchingly. "Do you even know my name?"

"I do not."

"It's Mattie Allend. Just call me "Mattie," not "Mrs. Allend," if you please. I've never been one for formality, and I've never had a husband. I'm just trying to look after my daughter." Mattie pointed at Millicent. "Millie knows nothing about what happened, aside from the fact that there was suddenly a hat and coat and scarf and walking stick she needed to hide away when she came home from babysitting the neighbor's brat. Is that clear? She's totally innocent. Of attempted murder at least. I suppose you've noticed that she's five months in the family way." I had observed that, but I had thought it indelicate to mention it.

"That was my doing, you know. I told her, Millie, you're a very pretty girl, but you're not very clever and husbands are more trouble than they're worth. If you want to be taken care of, you find yourself an older, prosperous career man with a wife and an

86

impeccable reputation, and you get yourself in the family way and make him take care of you and the kid. Not a nobleman, though. Those titled yobs are often flat broke, and they've no sense of paternal responsibility. I learned that the hard way with my first kid, my son. With Millie, I was cleverer. I found a Harley Street physician who liked me and didn't care much for his wife, but couldn't afford a scandal. Luckily for me Millie's the spitting image of him."

"That was your goal with Mr. Ivers?"

"It was. And a good plan, too. Ivers was besotted with her, and a few nights ago she told him he was about to become a father again. Well, he promised he'd take care of her, but she had to promise to never let his wife know about her or the baby. That was easy enough. She needs an income, not a scandal. It all would've been all right, but then that judge saw Ivers kissing her on the front stoop a few nights ago. The judge stopped his carriage and hurried out, but he was sick and slow. By the time he crossed the street Ivers was long gone, and Millie was on her way to babysit at the neighbor's. He must not have seen her leave, because the judge started pounding on the door, demanding to speak to her. He was making such a fuss, I felt I had to let him in. He hung up his coat and hat, and we had a nice, civilized talk for a while. He didn't approve of me, but I couldn't care less about a judge's opinion of my character unless I'm standing in the dock. Then he started insisting on going to

Ivers' wife and telling her everything. I told him not to be a woolly-headed fool, that he would ruin everything for Millie, but he insisted, he said Mrs. Ivers was his cousin, and he couldn't keep the news that her husband was going to have a baby out of wedlock from her. We argued, things got a bit heated, and I panicked a teensy bit and struck him with the ice pick. Next thing I know, I'm holding the handle in my hand, and he's stumbled out the door before I can get to him. I expected him to collapse and die right in front of the house. I've no idea how he managed to make his way to your home."

Mattie drained her glass. "Well, that's all, then. Millie came home an hour later and wanted to know what the clothing and cane were doing here, and I told her that at my age, a woman doesn't have to explain or justify her relationships with men. As she was gathering up everything, Ivers came back to the house, saying his friend hadn't come to dinner. He saw the clothes and cane, I took him aside, and told him for Millie's sake, he mustn't ask too many questions about Merridew. I implied that Millie might be unjustly blamed for his disappearance, so Ivers kept mum and paid the manservant a bit to do the same. So now you know everything. This was all for my daughter. I wanted to see her taken care of before I died. What'll happen to me now? It seems a waste of taxpayer money to pay for a trial. I'm going to a much more final courtroom soon enough."

Holmes gave her a long, penetrating gaze that was not completely devoid of sympathy. "I shall tell the authorities everything, and perhaps they shall be merciful."

They were. After a doctor confirmed that Mattie was not long for this world, Scotland Yard decided not to make an arrest, and the unfortunate woman died just over a week later in her own home. Merridew was placed in a nursing home, and passed away from complications connected to his cancer six months later. By the end, his memory grew more and more abominable, until he finally was unable to finish a sentence more than three words long without losing his train of thought. It was a tragic end to a reportedly brilliant legal mind.

Holmes did not expect a fee for his efforts, so it was a pleasant surprise when a substantial check arrived in the mail a week later. Its sender, Mr. Ivers, thanked us for finding out what had really happened to his friend, minimizing the fallout of the scandal, and asked us to protect the feelings of his wife and children. Holmes, caring little for the check but understanding the need to protect the innocent members of the Ivers family from embarrassment, agreed. And so, I write this account of the case solely for myself, and as soon as I finish, I will take it down to the vaults of Cox and Co. bank and lock it away in a battered tin dispatch-box, where it will rest in peace with dozens of other cases.

Intruders at Baker Street

"When a woman thinks that her house is on fire, her instinct is at once to rush to the thing which she values most. It is a perfectly overpowering impulse, and I have more than once taken advantage of it. In the case of the Darlington substitution scandal it was of use to me, and also in the Arnsworth Castle business. A married woman grabs at her baby; an unmarried one reaches for her jewel-box. "

– "A Scandal in Bohemia"

It is with some surprise and a bit of pleasure that I acknowledge that 221B Baker Street has become inextricably linked in the popular imagination with my friend Sherlock Holmes and myself. With the exception of certain politicians and members of the Royal Family, is there anybody else in England whose address is so well-known and iconic?

Recently, I realized that I had no idea who the inhabitants of 221B before my esteemed colleague were. We never received mail in any of their names, and Mrs. Hudson never mentioned them. I thought of asking our dear landlady about them, and then realized that I really had no interest in Baker Street B.H.– Before Holmes.

It was late January of 1887. After my marriage and my moving out of 221B, my visits to Holmes and the old homestead were far more infrequent than I would have liked. It was with great pleasure and some confusion that I received a note from Holmes one evening, telling me:

COME TO 221B THIS EVENING– CANCEL ALL OTHER PLANS.

–S.H.

If there was any trace of resentment in me at being ordered about by my friend, it was far overshadowed by my excitement at the prospect of another adventure with Sherlock Holmes. And so, after informing my wife that I would not be home for dinner and assisting a rather querulous old woman with her chilblains, I made my way to 221B to see my friend.

As I knocked on the door, I expected to see the familiar face of Mrs. Hudson greeting me. Instead, a much younger, taller, and lankier woman answered the door, speaking in a high-pitched Cockney voice that was utterly unlike anything that ever came out of Mrs. Hudson's.

"What're ya doing 'ere?" Mrs. Hudson would never have addressed a caller in such a manner.

"I'm here to see Sherlock Holmes," I informed her, wondering if Mrs. Hudson was ill and had recruited this person to handle her duties until she had recovered.

"'Oo's that?"

"Sherlock Holmes. The detective."

"Never 'eard h'of 'im. 'Oo're you?"

"I'm Doctor Watson."

"We don't need ya. No h'one's sick 'ere."

I was beginning to detect a touch of asperity creeping into my voice. "Now see here, I lived here for over five years, and–"

"Well, 'ow h'am h'I supposed t'know that? Hi've only been 'ere since this mornin', 'aven't h'I?"

My initial suspicions appeared to be confirmed. "Where is Mrs. Hudson?"

"Never 'eard h'of 'er."

"But this is her house. She's the landlady here."

"H'I don't know wot to tell you, Doc, but I never met a Mrs. 'Udson. No h'one mentioned 'er name h'all day. The Darlingtons 'ired me. This h'is their 'ouse."

I was completely blindsided. Could Mrs. Hudson have sold 221B without my knowledge? Who were the Darlingtons?

"Young lady, I realize that you cannot be aware of the history of a house where you have just become employed, but I can assure that that Mrs. Hudson has owned this building for years, and Mr. Sherlock Holmes is the well-known resident of these rooms. I should like to speak to him."

"'Oo can't. There's no wot's-'is-name 'ere. Just Mr. and Mrs. Darlington and 'is brother. And they've left orders not to be disturbed."

My patience with this woman had just reached its limit. "What is your name?"

"Hi'm Mrs. Turner. Least, h'I think h'I still h'am. "'Aven't seen him h'in h'a long, long time, but that don't mean my name changes back, does h'it?"

I was fairly certain that abandonment didn't necessitate a return to a woman's maiden name, but I was in no mood to ponder the intricacies of marriage law and customs. "Mrs. Turner, it is of the utmost importance that I should be allowed into 221B. Please allow me to come in. I shall make sure that you are not blamed for anything."

Mrs. Turner pursed her thin lips. "Well... h'I don't know..." Frustration started to seep into every fiber of my being, until I noticed that Mrs. Turner's right hand, dangling at her waist, was clenching and unclenching. Picking up on the hint, I rummaged in my coat pocket, extracted a few shiny coins, and slipped them into her outstretched fingers. With a triumphant smirk, Mrs. Turner stepped to one side, saying, "H'if h'anybody h'asks, you pushed past me."

"Fair enough." I took the stairs two at a time, and when I reached the door, I knocked on it. When no one answered after several moments, I seized the knob and entered. What I saw astounded me.

Three strangers, two men and a woman, were seated around the fire, surrounded by papers. Few of Holmes' possessions remained in their normal places, as the entire room looked as if it had been well rifled-through, though nothing was broken. The coal-scuttle had been dragged out to between the chairs, and all three invaders were smoking the cigars Holmes habitually kept there. From the large quantity of butts and ash littering some glass dishes that Holmes used for scientific experiments, and the emptied Persian slipper thrown into one corner of the room, they had nearly gone through Holmes' supply of tobacco.

"What are you doing here?" I asked.

At first, all three appeared unsettled. Then the larger of the two men stood up, attempting to appear calm and controlled. "I'm Roger Darlington. This is my home."

"It most certainly is not. This is Mr. Sherlock Holmes' home. I know this for a fact. You have no business being here."

"Nonsense! We've lived here for months!" This high-pitched declaration came from the woman, who was presumably Mrs. Darlington.

As I was aware that there was absolutely no truth to this statement, I knew at once that the three were liars. I was about to step forward and demand answers, when I abruptly realized that Holmes and Mrs. Hudson were very likely in danger. I immediately stepped out of the room and called down to the substitute housekeeper. "Mrs. Turner! Please go out immediately and fetch the nearest policeman. We need the authorities immediately." At first Mrs. Turner looked disinclined to leave, but I dipped into my pocket, selected the largest coin I could find, and tossed it down to her. Mrs. Turner sprinted out of the house the second the money touched her palm.

I whirled around to confront the interlopers, only to see a very large revolver pointed directly at me. The other man, not Roger Darlington, was pointing it at me. "Come back in here and don't make a sound," he snarled.

I had no choice but to reenter the room, and sat down when the man gestured me into a chair.

"Who are you?" he asked.

"I am Doctor John Watson. I am a close friend of Sherlock Holmes, and I lived at 221B with him for many years. I know that this is his home, I know that you have no business here, and now I wish to know who you are and what you are doing here." I was in no position to make demands, but I was in no mood to cower in front of these people.

The man with the gun made the most unpleasant smile I've ever seen. "You can call me Jack Darlington. You met Roger, and that's Eva there. And what we're doing here is none of your business."

I wasn't about to be cowed into silence, even if he was holding a gun. "Where are Holmes and Mrs. Hudson? Are they all right?"

"They're fine for now."

"Jack! Don't tell him any more!" Roger Darlington crossed the room. "We'll tie him up, and as soon as we can we'll put him with the others."

"Don't bother with that! Just take care of him!" If this was representative of Eva Darlington's character, I did not envy Roger for having this vicious creature as his wife.

"That would be most unwise," I informed them. "The walls here are definitely not soundproof. Do you see those bullet-holes in the wall there? Mr. Holmes is in the habit of practicing his pistol-shooting in this very room. Every time he has done so, he has drawn a great deal of unwanted attention. Pull that trigger, and a hundred angry neighbors will come rushing to 221B to complain. Can you fend off all of those people, with at most five bullets left in that gun? I should remind you, they all know who Holmes is, and they'll be wondering why you're here instead of him." This was a bluff. The neighbors have grown used to Holmes' pistol-shooting, and they stopped complaining about the noise years ago. Gunshots had long ceased to raise eyebrows in the neighborhood. But the Darlingtons didn't know that, and they appeared unsettled.

Presently, we heard the front door slamming. "That's the police," I informed them. "Can you really afford to risk a constable coming in and seeing you holding a gun?"

Roger tugged at Jack's elbow. "Go into the back room. We'll handle this." Jack obeyed, and disappeared into Holmes' bedroom just as Mrs. Turner and a policeman appeared in the doorway.

"Hello! What are you doing here?" Roger asked.

"This woman here says you needed a policeman," the officer of the law replied.

I didn't want to waste any time. "Sir! These people are criminals. This is the home of Mr. Sherlock Holmes, and they have kidnapped him and his landlady. I don't know what they're doing here, but there is a third member of this gang of crooks in the room back there, and he has a gun. Mrs. Turner, please run out and get as many policemen as you can! I will pay you for your efforts later."

Mrs. Turner turned to go, but the policeman stopped her. "Just a minute. Stay where you are while I ask a few questions. What's going on here?"

Roger Darlington affected a worried air. "I'm so glad you've come here. This man is clearly deranged. He burst into my home half an hour ago, rummaged through our things, and he refuses to leave."

Mrs. Darlington started sniffling. "He tried to take advantage of me! Fortunately my husband fought him off!"

"Did he now?" The policeman started growling at me.

"Sir, they are lying to you!"

"Are you calling that lady a liar?"

She's no lady, I thought to myself. I was starting to feel some trepidation. Perhaps something about the Darlingtons was more convincing to this policeman than I was, and I feared that unless I could completely win over this fellow, it was more likely than not that I would be dragged to the police station and kept there until I could prove that I was telling the truth. And in the meantime, what of Holmes and Mrs. Hudson? It might be hours, even days before I could vindicate myself, and for all I knew, my friends could be in mortal peril.

I decided to prove my story quickly. "Sir, I have worked with Inspector Lestrade of Scotland Yard on many occasions. He can verify the fact that this is truly Sherlock Holmes' residence."

There was a flicker of a response in the policeman's face, but it only lasted a moment. "I'm not familiar with an Inspector Lestrade. But it seems to me that this is a well-dressed couple. They don't look like burglars."

"Don't you see the mess in here? They've been searching this place!"

"That's true," Eva Darlington answered. "We're looking for... a little diamond that fell out of one of my rings. I know it must be somewhere in our home, but we don't know where. I don't want a precious gemstone to be thrown out or lost forever, so we're performing a careful and methodical search. I admit things are a bit messy, but we'll straighten everything out once we find my diamond."

I couldn't believe it. That mutton-headed oaf in a helmet was nodding. "That sounds reasonable to me."

"Don't you see they changed their story? First they lied and said I rummaged through their things, then they said they're looking for a mythical diamond. They're clearly lying!" If the young bobby heard a word I said, he didn't show any signs of having done so.

Roger Darlington seized the opportunity. "This man is clearly not in his right mind. He's been blathering on and on about his imaginary friend and we cannot get him to leave, and he's threatened my wife. I'd be very grateful if you could be kind enough to take him down to the police station."

"I'll do that, sir. Sorry that you've been troubled by this man." The fool put his hand on my arm. "If you'll come with me, mister!"

"Just a minute!" I whipped Holmes' letter out of my pocket. "Look at the return address on this envelope! Sherlock Holmes! 221B Baker Street!"

This stopped him. He stared at the envelope for a moment, and for the first time in a while I had hope that I might be able to convince him that I was in the right.

"He probably wrote that himself," Eva Darlington scoffed.

I have never felt such feelings of loathing towards a woman as I did at that moment towards Eva Darlington.

"Yes, he probably did, didn't he?" The moron's face actually brightened.

I was reminding myself that it would be unwise to descend to the use of physical violence to extract myself from this situation when inspiration struck me. "Look here, the Darlingtons claim to have lived here for years. Can they produce a single piece of mail with their names on it that was delivered to this address?"

The look of horror on the Darlingtons' faces told me that the tide was turning in my favor. My eye wandered over to the fireplace, and I spotted my salvation. Turning back to the policeman, I confidently informed him, "These frauds claim they've never heard of Sherlock Holmes and that I've only been here a short while. Take a look at the center of the wooden mantelpiece. You see that jack-knife sticking out of it? Look at all of the envelopes that have been pierced with that blade. Take a good look at them, and see who they're addressed to. And if you still doubt me, check the postmarks. You'll see that they were delivered at least a couple of days ago, long before the Darlingtons claimed that I first darkened their doorstep."

The policeman shuffled over to the fireplace, extracted the jack-knife with some difficulty, and peered down at the name written on the envelopes in the addressee section. "Mr. Sherlock Holmes," he muttered with a look of pure incredulity on his face.

Before I could cry out a warning, Roger Darlington seized the fireplace poker and swung it through the air, striking the policeman on the back of the neck.

It looked to me as if he'd moderated the force of his blow, just enough to knock the man out, but not enough to kill. Mrs. Turner started screaming, and I moved towards her, but Eva Darlington practically flew across the room and knocked Mrs. Turner to the floor, ripping the cap of Mrs. Turner's head and stuffing it into her mouth.

I made a very quick decision. I could try to disarm Roger Darlington, or I could try to save Mrs. Turner from Eva Darlington. But whichever Darlington I attacked (and my sense of honor reeled at the thought of fighting a woman), there was another factor in play. The third Darlington, Jack. At any moment, he could burst out of Holmes's room with a loaded gun.

I chafed at the prospect of retreating, but I realized that I had no choice but to flee and gather reinforcements as soon as possible to rescue the policeman and Mrs. Turner. I rushed out the door as fast as I could, realizing that Roger Darlington was running after me, brandishing the poker.

Practically flying down the stairs, I sailed out the front door and down the street. After sprinting another hundred yards, I became aware that Roger Darlington was no longer chasing me. I sought out familiar faces and competent members of law enforcement as quickly as I could, and a little over ten minutes later I returned to 221B with a passel of allies in tow.

The policeman was still lying in front of the fireplace and I confirmed that he was merely unconscious and not in mortal danger. There was a nasty lump on Mrs. Turner's forehead, almost certainly inflicted by the brutish Roger Darlington's poker. Mrs. Turner was not badly injured, and as I examined her, one of her eyes fluttered open and she muttered, "'Oo wouldn't be thinkin' about taking your coins back from me while hi'm h'out cold, would'oo?"

I smiled. Despite my initial misgivings, I was starting to like Mrs. Turner.

The policemen, far more competent than their knocked-out colleague, searched 221B, and then the rest of the building. There was no trace of any of the Darlingtons. Holmes and Mrs. Hudson were nowhere to be found, either.

The injured policeman and Mrs. Turner were taken to the hospital for observation, and I started searching for some clue as to why the Darlingtons had installed themselves at 221B, and what they might have done with my friends. As I sorted through the papers that had been strewn about, I realized that they had completely torn apart Holmes' index of assorted people and subjects. The index was so vast and comprehensive that it was impossible for me, who had only had a brief glimpse of its contents now and then, to identify what, if anything, was missing.

The police officers and my other colleagues had left, confident that I was safe on my own. I spent the better part of an hour poring through 221B, not knowing exactly what I was looking for, but hoping for the best. Finally, I thought to look inside the wastepaper basket, and discovered a small paper bag with the name "Bunder's Bonbons" stamped on it. Inside were a few fragments of a sickly-floral-smelling hard candy. I had never known Holmes to partake in that sort of sweet, and after a minute's reflection, decided that it was the closest thing to a clue that I had.

A few inquiries, and I had the address of "Bunder's Bonbons." I decided not to inform the police, as I had no solid proof that this was anything more than a scrap of litter that had inadvertently blown into the house, and Holmes had disposed of it.

Still, if there was any chance at all that it might lead me to my missing friends...

I hired a carriage and asked the driver to speed as fast as humanly possible to my home, where I informed my wife of my destination and instructed her to call the police if I did not get in touch with her within three hours. After making sure that my service revolver was fully loaded and securely in my pocket with a supply of additional ammunition, I returned to my carriage and requested that the driver travel more quickly than he had ever done before in his life.

In half an hour I had reached Bunder's Bonbons, a seedy little shop in a run-down part of London. After instructing the carriage-driver to wait for me, I stepped inside, where an acne-scarred young man slouched behind the counter.

"Can I get anything for you, sir?"

I sized him up, and decided to confront him with a blunt question. "Do you know anybody by the name of Darlington?"

"Sure, they rent part of our basement. Why do you ask?"

I was astounded. Part of me expected this young man to be in league with the Darlingtons, and I hadn't expected him to be so obliging with his information. Wary of a trap, I asked him to describe the Darlingtons. His words exactly matched the three people I had seen. When I inquired as to why they rented rooms in their basement, he shrugged, and replied:

"They say they need the space to house some things of theirs. We've got more room than we can use, and we need the money, so it's a good deal for us. Would you be interested in renting some space down there? I can give you a good price."

I expressed an interest and asked to be shown down there. I made sure the young man went first. He seemed harmless enough, but I was prepared for a sudden attack, so as we made our way down the rickety, dark stairs into the moldy basement, I kept my hand on my revolver, just in case I was being led into an ambush.

The passageway was quite narrow, and I was trying to keep my coat from brushing against the stone walls, which even in the dim lantern light were covered with dust and grit and cobwebs. A few doors were spaced out on either side, but my guide led me to the very end of the corridor, to the only door that was fastened shut with a lock.

"I don't have the key," he informed me. "But this is the Darlingtons' storage room. Can I show you one of the other empty rooms?"

Before I could answer, I heard a couple of thumps behind the door. "What was that?"

"Couldn't tell you. Maybe it's rats. There were a couple of big ones a couple of months ago that got into the peppermint rock. I thought I got rid of 'em, but you never know with rats now, do you?"

My instincts told me that the noise in question wasn't being made by rodents. I pushed past the young man and rapped on the door. I heard more thumps in reply, and despite the fact that I used none of Holmes' famous methods of deduction, I was quite certain that I knew what was behind that door.

"Holmes! Mrs. Hudson! Get away from the door if you can!" I withdrew my service revolver, advised my young colleague to cover his ears, positioned the gun, and shot open the lock. The door remained slightly stuck, so I planted my feet, delivered a mighty kick to door, and sent it swinging backwards.

A pair of muffled voices came out of the darkness. Taking the lantern, I inched into the room, and found Holmes and Mrs. Hudson lying on the floor, separately bound and gagged. The knots were a challenge, but fortunately my young associate lent me the use of his pocket knife. I cut Mrs. Hudson free first, and it only took a few more moments to release Holmes.

My friends were unharmed, but sore and dirty, and it took a bit of massaging to get the blood flowing back into their legs, allowing them to rise to their feet. We all made our way upstairs, and after Holmes and Mrs. Hudson had seen to some pressing needs and cleaned themselves up a bit, I started to recount my experiences that evening to them. After just a few minutes, Mrs. Hudson was shocked at hearing of strangers in her house, and highly suspicious of Mrs. Turner, so she insisted on returning to 221B immediately in order to examine how much damage the Darlingtons had done. I placed her in the carriage and sent her back home, while Holmes and I made our way to a nearby public house for some refreshment.

Holmes helped himself to a plate of dark brown bread and very pale cheese with rather more delight than I felt this simple fare deserved, though I could understand his hunger. I explained my experiences in more detail as Holmes ate and we both drank, and by the time I finished, not a crumb of bread or a speck of cheese remained on the plate.

"I must congratulate you," Holmes told me right after he downed the remaining contents of his glass. "You have performed admirably tonight. I freely admit that you have distinguished yourself far better than I have this evening."

"Holmes, what happened to you? Who are the Darlingtons and why did they take over 221B?

"This will take a bit of time. I suggest that you take a moment to write out a note informing your wife that you have found us and everybody is quite all right, and that she shouldn't worry if you don't come home tonight until quite late. I believe I see an old acquaintance of mine in that corner over there who will be happy to serve as a messenger in exchange for five shillings."

Realizing this was a good idea, I followed Holmes' suggestion, and noticed that Holmes was scribbling a note of his own. I was about to ask him what he was writing, but I reasoned that he would tell me as soon as he was prepared to tell me. As soon as the messages were written and sent on their ways, Holmes returned to the table with another pair of drinks and leaned back in his chair. "I shall begin by answering your second question first. The Darlingtons are a family of con artists, two brothers and one brother's wife. I'm quite certain that Darlington is not their real name, and the first names Roger, Eva, and Jack are just as likely to be spurious, but that does not matter at present. For the moment, we can use those titles. The Darlingtons specialize in a very specific branch of fraud. They are professional substitutes."

"What on earth are professional substitutes?"

"The word "imposters" would be just as apt a term, I suppose. The Darlington collect their ill-gotten gains by pretending to be other people, and they insert themselves into unsuspecting people's lives in order to enrich themselves at others' expense. They find prominent people whose faces aren't very well-known, and assume their identities in order to get ahold of as much money as possible. They like to specialize in titled individuals living abroad. Lord and Lady Eggmere have lived in India or nearly twenty years, and the Darlingtons posed as the Eggmeres for a few days, claiming that they were back for a brief visit to take care of business matters. They wound up cleaning out one of the Eggmere's bank accounts, and took out several enormous loans from both respectable financial institutions and shady dealers in the Eggmere's names. As soon as suspicions started being raised, they went into hiding. In another case, a Mr. and Mrs. Totnurse left some valuable heirlooms at a jeweler's to be reset while they were off for a month-long holiday in Paris. A couple of days before the real Totnurses returned, the Darlingtons arrived at the jeweler's, disguised as the Totnurses, and collected all the necklaces and rings. They have been in business for over three years, and they are very careful to space out their crimes with four to six-month breaks between them, so as to avoid suspicion. I believe they have accumulated a considerable fortune by now."

"How did you learn about them?"

"One of their victims is a member of an extremely prominent family, who was temporarily exiled to Kenya for some potentially embarrassing indiscretions. It was hoped that after a couple of years of managing a coffee farm, this reckless young man could be allowed back into polite London society. However, one of the Darlingtons pretended to be him, and visited some of the most infamous moneylenders around, taking out loans that ran into tens of thousands of pounds. Well, the family, who for reasons I am sure you will understand I will not name even to you, worried that even though their prodigal son was completely innocent in this matter, that any sort of scandal attaching to his name might lead to an extended delay in the errant young man's return to England, where he would make a prudent marriage to some well-off young woman. The family in question, though very respectable, is in somewhat limited financial circumstances, and they lack the liquid assets to pay off the debts the Darlingtons racked up recently."

"Surely the family would not plunge themselves into bankruptcy in order to pay off loans taken out by criminals under false pretenses."

"You forget the delicate bubble reputations of high society, Watson. In these circles, the slightest connection to a crime is a most fearful scandal, even if one is called into court solely as a witness. The merest connection with wrongdoing is to be avoided at all costs. If false loans were taken out in the errant scion's name, it might potentially affect the family's credit, and they need to take out a perfectly respectable bank loan in order to pay for the repairs to the roof of their family estate. Not only that, but the loan sharks do not care one whit for the fact that the person who borrowed money in the young man's name was an impostor. The loans were taken out four months ago, and they are accumulating interest by the week. The moneylenders want to be paid back immediately, and they're willing to make quite the fuss if they don't get recompensed sooner rather than later."

"That hardly seems fair."

"It isn't. That is why the eldest daughter of the family in question came to me, asking me to help them track down the criminals and retrieve the money if possible. That way, the ill-gotten funds could go back to the moneylenders, and the family would be willing to swallow the costs of the additional interest payments."

"So what happened?"

"I interviewed a handful of the loan sharks, and they managed to provide me with some useful information from snippets of small talk the imposter had made with them. He'd mentioned lunching at the Savoy, and when I spoke to the maître d' and gave him a description of the man and his clothing, he told me that the man dined there regularly. I frequented the Savoy for a few days, until the maître d' pointed out that the man in question had returned. After he had finished his meal, I followed him to the house he shared with his brother and sister-in-law. I wondered if they kept their ill-gotten gains at their home– after all, they could not deposit their stolen funds into a bank without drawing unwanted attention, so I fancied that I would try to make them retrieve their hidden cache of loot through a ruse. I wrote a quick note and sent it to you, thinking that I might need your help later in the evening. After surreptitiously looking in the window and finding all three of the Darlingtons there, I decided to climb up to the roof and block the top of their chimney. It didn't take long for the house to fill with smoke, but my hopes of seeing the three of them run out of the building carrying enormous sacks of stolen cash were dashed. I did notice that Mrs. Darlington was clasping her jewel-box close to her heart. I suspect that the box was filled with illicitly-obtained jewelry. The larger of the Darlingtons noticed the plank of wood I'd placed over their chimney, and immediately started climbing up the roof to remove it. While he was up there, he must have seen me crouched in the hiding place that was not as secure as I'd hoped. When he climbed down, he slowly ambled in my direction, calling out something about buying some cigarettes, and then lunged at where I was hiding, catching me off guard and pinioning me. I might have been able to fight him off, but before I could do anything the other two Darlingtons surrounded me. Mrs. Darlington identified me at once– how she recognized me I'm not sure, but I suspect that she read one of your colorful accounts of my investigations. They knew I was after them, and when Mrs. Darlington asked what they were going to do with me, one of the brothers growled "This!" and struck me firmly on the back of the

113

neck. When I regained consciousness, I was hopelessly tied up in a room with no light and no way of figuring out where I was. After an hour or so, the door opened and the infernal family threw a similarly bound and gagged Mrs. Hudson into the room with me. With the light that the Darlingtons brought, I could see that the room was filled with several large steamer trunks. From the way the Darlingtons handled some of them, I suspect that some were filled with cash, and others were filled with heavier items. At a guess, I'd say that one of them held the equipment they used to create the false identification papers they used in their impostures, and others contained jewelry and other valuable items they'd stolen over the years. They said nothing to us, and I had no idea if they intended to have someone come to rescue us as some point, or if they simply decided to leave us there and let us die of starvation. I spent hours trying to free myself, gaining nothing but a few rope burns in the process. Then you came by and saved the day, my dear fellow, and for that you have my eternal gratitude. Thank you."

I savored the complement for a moment. Eventually, my curiosity triumphed over my need to bask in this rare bit of praise. "Why did they move into 221B? What did they hope to accomplish by that? And why did they hire Mrs. Turner?"

"They must have learned my address from your surprisingly popular accounts of our exploits, and they may have thought it wise to look through my belongings to see if I'd left some notes to tell them just how much I knew about their crimes, and how safe it was for them to remain in England. They are sufficiently inured to violence to knock out innocent people and to threaten them with firearms, but to the best of my knowledge and belief, they have never actually killed anybody, and they may not have the stomachs to torture someone for information, either. They probably figured it was easier and more effective to search my rooms than to interrogate me. As you told me, Watson, they were rummaging through the contents of my comprehensive index. When they discovered it, they realized that it could potentially be a gold mine of information for them, as it contained valuable information on many people, including potential new victims for them to impersonate. In any case, they didn't know if I'd told anybody about the location of their home, so they decided it was not safe for them to return there. At some point, Mrs. Hudson caught them and knew they were up to no good, so they incapacitated her and smuggled her to their hideout. I dare say they selected the basement of the candy store to hold their ill-gotten gains because it was cheap to rent, the owners are not inquisitive, there's a back door leading to an alley that they could use to sneak in and out, and the basement of a sweet shop is the last place the police would look for a fortune in ill-gotten gains. The Darlingtons knew that they needed a little peace and quiet to sort through my index, so they quickly found a housekeeper who would turn away anybody coming to consult with me, and bring them some refreshment as they needed it."

"So now what will happen?"

"As you saw, I wrote a note that my acquaintance will deliver to Lestrade. They know that their home, their hideaway, and 221B are no longer secure for them. They retrieved several large trunks, and they cannot simply lug them around. Unless they have another hiding-place, which I think is unlikely, they will head for a port and set sail overseas, probably to Canada or the United States, though I cannot rule out some other location. Scotland Yard is best equipped to track them down, though we should make ourselves available to the authorities in case they need us to identify the Darlingtons."

Holmes was completely correct. Within two hours, Lestrade's men had caught the Darlingtons aboard a ship scheduled to set sail for Nova Scotia in the morning. In addition to the trunks filled with money and valuables, they found many of Holmes' notes from his index. They were clearly planning to continue their schemes by exploiting some prominent Canadians. Though they'd spent a fair portion of the stolen cash, the victims of the impostures all received the lion's share of their stolen goods back, and Holmes was able to prevent a scandal from impugning the good name of a prominent family.

Holmes and Mrs. Hudson suffered no lasting ill-effects from their confinement, and after interviewing Mrs. Turner, Holmes took a liking to her, and over the coming years, Mrs. Hudson routinely hired Mrs. Turner to take over her duties when she was out of town visiting relatives.

The young policeman who'd nearly sided with the Darlingtons over me spent a few days under observation in the hospital, but suffered no ill-effects. He had little talent for his profession, but he had influential relatives, so he was swiftly promoted to a supervisory position where he could do little harm.

I spent much of the next day helping Holmes straighten up his rooms, and after several hours of tidying, sorting, and re-alphabetizing Holmes' index, 221B looked exactly as it did before the Darlingtons took over the place. As I looked around 221B, I realized that not only could I not imagine anybody else living in this place, I never wanted anyone other than Holmes to live there, either.

The Heinous Half-Crowns

As I climbed the steps at 221B Baker Street that dreary autumn afternoon in 1899, I had no inkling that an adventure from a decade earlier would be continuing that evening. My work that day consisted of dealing with a half-dozen people with singularly unpleasant physical complaints, and I was looking forward to a quiet night in front of the fire with a hot dinner and a good book. My tiredness had made me forget that my long association with Sherlock Holmes meant that adventure could strike at any moment, especially when I was in most need of peace and quiet.

Just as I reached the second-highest step of the stairs, Holmes opened the door and met me with an excited gleam in his eye. "Evening, dear fellow. Are you hoping for a restful, relaxing evening? If so, you may want to go back down the stairs and visit your club. If you do choose to come inside our rooms, you will undoubtedly be drawn into a case that will take up the majority of the night, and you may not be able to get any sleep for quite a while."

If my wits had been sharper, I would have given Holmes a curt nod and turned on my heels. Instead, I walked straight into our rooms, barely hearing Holmes say, "Delighted you made the decision you did, Watson."

After I hung up my coat and hat and turned around, I became aware of a mountainous presence in the room. Holmes's brother Mycroft was sitting in our most comfortable chair, with the remains of a plate of Mrs. Hudson's rock cakes at his side. Mycroft met my gaze and asked. "Hello, Watson. A woman with boils, twins with colic, a man who cut himself shaving and got infected, and an elderly gentleman with a case of phlebitis. Am I correct?"

I was about to confirm his deductions, ask how he knew about my patients' complaints, and inform him that he had missed the middle-aged man with gout, but then I realized that patient confidentiality issues prevented me from saying anything, and told him so. Mycroft smiled, turned to his right, and said, "You see, Mr. Dacres? I told you that Doctor Watson can be trusted to be discreet."

I hadn't noticed Mr. Dacres until then. There could not have been a sharper physical contrast between the two men. Dacres was a tiny man, no more than five foot two, and he looked as if he'd never had a proper meal in his life. His voice was raspy and wheezy, and I immediately got the impression that he had a very low opinion of me. "How do we know that the doctor won't put everything he hears into one of his tawdry stories?"

Before I could take issue with his use of the word "tawdry," Mycroft informed him, "I can assure you that Doctor Watson has never published a word that hasn't been approved of by me. I can name no fewer than thirteen cases connected to the British national interest where I have asked Watson to refrain from publishing a story, and he has always complied."

Dacres fixed a suspicious glare upon me, creating the impression that if an angel came down from Heaven and told him to trust me, he would still view me with suspicion. While I appreciated his need to be cautious, I was starting to feel a bit insulted when Holmes stepped in to defend my honor.

"Mr. Dacres, either you can decide to trust Watson, or you can kindly leave my rooms at once. If you wish my help, you must accept Watson's assistance as well. The choice is yours."

Despite Holmes' declaration, Dacres still seemed reluctant, until Mycroft slapped his beefy hand against the end table. "Enough prevarication, Dacres! We have an urgent matter at hand. Will you introduce yourself, or shall I?" When Dacres sulked, Mycroft groaned and turned to me. "Mr. Dacres is part of a department of British Intelligence that technically does not exist. The handful of individuals who know about it refer to it as the MPS. The Ministry for the Prevention of Scandal. For the last two decades, whenever a prominent member of the Government or the Royal Family does something reprehensible, Mr. Dacres jumps in to hush it up completely."

"Is he usually successful?" Holmes asked.

Mycroft shrugged. "About sixty percent of the time."

Holmes leaned back in his chair. "How much taxpayer money does the MPS spend covering up scandals?"

As Mycroft drummed his fingers, I could see the numbers and calculations flashing across his eyes. After a couple of moments, he pronounced, "About two million guineas a year. We usually chalk it up to war expenses." He turned to me. "Do you remember reading in the newspapers about how we had to send troops to Mount Kosciuszko last year to quell an uprising?"

"I did."

"There was no war there. We simply picked that area because it was far away and no one was going to visit it and discover that everything was perfectly peaceful. I wrote the dispatches from the frontlines myself under a pseudonym, and we gave a couple of dozen soldiers we could trust a handful of medals each in exchange for telling fictional war stories about the Battle of Mount Kosciuszko in public places. We needed to invent that military intervention in order to square the books after the MPS hushed up an incident involving three minor members of the Royal Family, two tiaras from the Crown Jewels where the diamonds had been removed and replaced with rhinestones, and two dead tigers at the London Zoo."

I had so many questions to ask, but Dacres was determined to leave my curiosity unquenched. "That's enough!" he barked.

"How many times have I told you never to speak to me in a tone like that?" Mycroft asked calmly. "Still, I can understand why Dacres might be reluctant to reveal have the details of the latest scandal   revealed   to   the   public."

"Thank you, Mycroft."

"I can understand your feelings, Dacres, but I don't agree with them in the least. If my brother is to help you out of a problem of your own making, he's going to need to know exactly why he's being called into the case." Mycroft continued, projecting his voice over Dacres' shrill protestations. "A week ago, a young man working as a secretary for a back-bencher Member of Parliament was kidnapped. His abductors requested a hundred pounds for his safe return, in gold or silver coins. Now, that young fellow was worth a ten-pound ransom at most, but unfortunately his mother is a very… *close friend* of several Cabinet members and some prominent members of the House of Lords. She threatened to kick up a nasty fuss if her darling boy wasn't returned home immediately and in perfect condition, so the MPS was called in to settle the matter."

"Is the man all right?" Holmes asked.

"Perfectly fine. The problem was with the ransom money. Dacres has been spending the public funds like water lately, and given his subpar performance record and the fact that he recently wasted over a million guineas on a failed attempt to cover up an unfortunate indiscretion involving the ambassadors of four other countries, for the first time in recent memory, Dacres found himself devoid of funds. The Victorian Age was excellent for his business, wasn't it, Dacres? But alas, there's an unfortunate permissive streak running through society lately, enough to make members of the government start putting profits over principles. In any case, after a string of spectacular failures, Dacres' name is mud, and they're no longer willing to give him *carte blanche* for anything less than a scandal that will bring down the monarchy."

Holmes sighed. "I'm not inclined to use my investigative powers to save the rich and powerful from embarrassment, unless there's a compelling national interest to do so."

"This is a different situation," Mycroft explained. "The kidnapping victim is home safe and his mother is no longer threatening to reveal her life's story. The problem is the ransom money and the need to retrieve it."

"Why are you so concerned about a mere hundred pounds in coins?" I asked.

"It's not the amount of money, it's the specific coins that are a matter of national security." After adjusting his position in his chair, Mycroft continued. "Surely you remember the case that you dubbed "The Adventure of the Engineer's Thumb?"

That grisly case was forever etched in my memory. "Of course."

"You recall, then, that though my brother managed to track down the location of the criminals' home base, the criminals were never brought to justice. At least… that's the narrative that I wanted you to tell the world." Mycroft gave Holmes a little nod, and Holmes gave his sibling a thin-lipped smile.

I turned to my friend. "Holmes, is there more to that story?"

Holmes chuckled. "I'm afraid I withheld the final chapter of that adventure from you, my dear fellow. Did you never think it odd that I failed to make more of an effort to track down the criminals?"

I made no reply. I was concerned that I might say something to offend Holmes. Truth be told, I *had* wondered why the investigation had stopped at that point, but when Holmes seemed content to let the matter rest at that point, I set my personal concerns to one side, and allowed myself to believe that the "Adventure of the Engineer's Thumb" ended with us looking over the burnt-out remains of a house.

I don't know if Holmes was able to follow my train of thought, as he often has in the past. Whatever he guessed about my musings, he continued, saying, "Within an hour of the conversation that ended your colorful recounting of the case, a young man who I recognized as one of Mycroft's many emissaries bumped into me on the street, slipping a note into my hand as he passed on by. Upon reading it, I discovered that it was from Mycroft, telling me not to pursue the villains, and that a team of operatives under his supervision were in the process of tracking them down, where they would face justice, though not in the courts."

"Are you saying that they were executed without trial?" I asked, unable to keep the indignation out of my voice.

"Of course not!" Mycroft snorted. "Whatever you may think about the secret workings of the British government, I can assure you that the rule of law is always followed... except in certain emergencies. In any case, the man you knew as Colonel Lysander Stark and his confederates were captured two days after the events that ended your narrative, Doctor. We rounded up the gang and confiscated all of their counterfeit half-crowns. Given their skill at duplicating the coin of the realm, we offered them a special deal. Either they could go to trial and almost certainly be convicted for counterfeiting– I didn't threaten them with execution for the death of Jeremiah Hayling, the young hydraulic engineer who was almost certainly murdered by Stark and his gang, as we didn't have his body, and empty intimidation would have made me appear to be a paper tiger– or they could accept a special deal where they would be imprisoned in a slightly more comfortable prison in exchange for working with the government to use their counterfeiting skills to serve the interests of Britain."

"Do you mean finding ways to protect British currency from counterfeiting?"

"No, Doctor. To help us find ways to counterfeit the currency of other nations. If we can demonstrate to our rivals that we possess the ability to replicate their money, it gives us a distinct advantage in various negotiations."

"I beg your pardon!"

"You are shocked, Doctor, but I can assure you, by finding inexpensive substitutes for gold and silver, and duplicating the molds for coins, we have prevented ten wars in as many years and have managed to set up countless favorable trade agreements that have solidified England's prosperity."

I was far from convinced that the ends justified the means, and my face must have betrayed my moral outrage, but before I could speak again, Holmes reentered the conversation. "By the way, Watson, you may be wondering about what happened to the young woman in the case. As she had helped save Mr. Hatherley and was more of a hostage than an active participant in the counterfeiting ring, Mycroft's associates gave her a new identity and a fresh start in one of the colonies. She is, I understand, quite content with her second chance at life."

This was welcome news to me, though it did not thoroughly quench my indignation. "So the Colonel and his gang are now living a comparatively comfortable life behind bars, finding ways to replicate the coinage of other countries?"

"Yes. The talents of evil men can be redirected to serve the greater good of the nation." Mycroft cleared his throat. "Dacres, would you care to continue the story and explain how your latest attempt to prevent scandalizing the British public went wrong?"

Dacres made a face like he'd just swallowed strychnine, and Mycroft continued as if he hadn't noticed his associate's expression. "As you will recall, Dacres needed a hundred pounds in gold or silver coins for the ransom. Had he asked a week earlier, the Treasury would have provided him with what he requested with no questions asked. Unfortunately, a recent report on the incredible losses the nation has suffered due to his extraordinarily expensive cover-ups has itself caused a minor scandal and it's costing the government a small fortune to keep it out of the papers. Therefore, the powers that be were debating a plan to have the money deducted from his salary."

"It was completely unfair! I wasn't to blame for the plans not turning out the way I'd hoped! Why should I be forced to pay for mistakes beyond my control? And time was of the essence! By the time those bureaucrats were agreed on how to make me the victim, the mother of that dratted kidnapping victim could have endangered the reputations of some of the most prominent members of our government! I am a man of action, and I did what I had to do in order to save the nation."

Mycroft was not impressed by Dacres' outburst. "You could have gone to the bank and withdrawn a hundred pounds of your own money. I've seen your account total. Your savings could withstand the blow."

"It's the principle!" Dacres squeaked. "If I paid out of my own pocket this time, they'd keep making me fund projects out of my own pocket until I went bankrupt! And in any case, I'm not to blame–"

"Yes, yes, so you've said." Mycroft sounded horribly bored. "So Dacres, in need of a hundred pounds in silver or gold coins, and having insufficient funds in petty cash, decided to loot a storage room in the building where he works, one that just happened to contain several chests full of the counterfeit half-crowns produced by Colonel Stark's gang."

"It was one of my secretaries' ideas. It seemed like an elegant solution," Dacres quipped. "Pay off the criminals with phony money, and possibly we could track them down when they tried to spend it and we caught them with the fake coins."

"Yes, but as some of my spies have recently informed me, the goal wasn't to make a hundred pounds. The kidnappers must have coached your secretary to make that suggestion. Their real objective was to obtain a considerable sample of the nickel and tin amalgam that Colonel Stark's gang used to replicate the silver used in half-crowns. That's the trickiest part of counterfeiting coins. You need to use a metal that looks just like real silver and weighs approximately the same amount as silver, but which only costs a fraction of the price of silver. That was the particular genius of the Stark gang. By combining nickel, tin, and a few other substances, they were able to create an alloy that replicated real silver so closely that only time-consuming laboratory tests could prove definitively that it was not actually silver." Mycroft grimaced. "It is my belief that a foreign power wishes to gain an advantage over us by gaining the ability to replicate our silver currency. I've been aware of a project along these lines for some time, but our enemies have never been able to come up with a convincing substitute for silver. Somehow, they must have found out about the Stark counterfeit half-crowns and organized this kidnapping and the subsequent manipulation of Dacres in order to gain possession of eight hundred coins made out of the silver substitute alloy. That would be enough to run sufficient tests to determine the formula and replicate it, thereby allowing one of England's enemies to gain the upper hand with us in negotiations and possibly disrupt our economy."

Holmes finally appeared interested in this situation. "So you wish for me to track down the counterfeit half-crowns before they can be melted down and analyzed by a rival country?"

"Precisely."

"I don't see how you can expect to be of much use, Mr. Holmes," Dacres sulked. "After all, by this point, the villains may already have spirited the fake coins out of the country and into the hands of whoever recruited them."

"Possibly, possibly." Holmes performed a few quick calculations. "Given the weight of a standard half-crown, eight hundred of them would weigh a little less than twenty-five pounds... I am not using the troy ounce system because we're referring to the alloy here and not actual silver. Given the size and weight, it should be fairly easy to smuggle. Coins could be stacked inside thick walking sticks, slipped into hidden compartments in luggage, or melted down and molded into any shape desired. Indeed, it would be nearly impossible to track down." His eyes flashed. "I need to see if the kidnappers have left any evidence of their location. Do you have the ransom letter?"

"I do." Mycroft handed an envelope to his brother.

Holmes picked up the envelope by one corner and carried it over to his laboratory table. He removed the letter and scrutinized it with his magnifying lens. After several minutes of examination, Dacres lost his patience.

"What the devil are you doing? You're not going to find anything of interest on that note. I've already looked over it."

"Perhaps you should've looked under certain portions of the letter." Holmes said, peeling one of the words that had been pasted on to the paper off with a pair of tweezers. "This slip of newsprint here provides a valuable clue. It's a larger piece, but I believe it must have been cut from the second page, because the letters are a considerably bigger than the standard headline. I suspect that they came from the title of the newspaper. Even through the thin layer of glue, I can tell that the letters are "PSW.""

"That's an unusual combination of letters," I remarked.

"Indeed, Watson. From the font, I would guess that the letters come from the town of "Ipswich," and that this is from a local newspaper there. The Ipswich paper isn't easily found in London, so whoever used this paper may have just been passing through Ipswich and bought a paper, but more likely than not, he has ties to Ipswich."

"Sounds reasonable to me, Holmes," I agreed.

"From the way these papers are cut, I can tell that the person holding the scissors is right-handed."

"That hardly narrows it down," Dacres blustered.

"No, you're quite right there. But these indentations on the undersides of the cut-out words indicate that a heavy, flat object was pressed repeatedly against all of these slips of paper while they were cut. It suggests that the person doing the cutting wore a large ring, possibly a signet ring. Furthermore, I can find a small clipping of hair trapped inside the glue under this word here. It's steel gray. If this letter was prepared a week ago at the time of the kidnapping, the person who cut these letters is a gray-haired man who had his hair cut about a week ago."

"Thousands of men fit that description, Holmes!"

"True, Mr. Dacres, very true. But right now only one man who fits the profile of the person I just described interests me."

"Oh?" Dacres was perspiring. "And who is that?"

Holmes strode casually up to the agitated civil servant. "You yourself, Mr. Dacres. You are right-handed, I can tell from how you're mopping your brow with your handkerchief right now. Your hair is a metallic gray, and it's clearly been cut sometime in the last week, give or take a couple of days. But the most notable point is that signet ring on your right hand."

Dacres tried to yank his hand away, but Holmes gripped his right wrist firmly and twisted the large signet ring from his finger. After a moment's study under the magnifying lens, Holmes smiled grimly. "As I suspected. Traces of glue."

"That's sealing wax!" Dacres spluttered.

"True, there is wax on the seal, but there's glue as well, and a chemical analysis will match it to the glue on the letter. Watson, consult my copy of *Who's Who*. See if our guest here has any family connections to Ipswich."

"I can spare you the trouble," Mycroft replied. "Dacres' family estate is in Ipswich. He goes there most weekends."

Dacres began squirming in his chair, and the blood was draining rapidly from his face. With every twitch, I expected him to jump up and sprint for the door in an attempt to escape, so I rose and made my way between him and the door. Looking at the wretched man, I was pretty certain that the expression on his face radiated guilt.

Holmes' gaze was locked onto Dacres. Without warning, Dacres suddenly became very still, and his right hand started inching its way into his jacket. "None of that!" Holmes shouted, lunging at Dacres, who was momentarily frozen by the sharpness of my friend's exclamation. Holmes's hands gripped Dacres' wrist tightly, and with a quick twist, he extracted a small pistol from Dacres' hand.

Sinking back into his chair, Holmes pocketed the pistol, and remarked, "That's as close to a confession as one can get without the culprit actually admitting his guilt. You were right, my dear brother."

"Right?" I asked. "Holmes, are you saying that Mycroft suspected Dacres from the beginning?"

"Of course, Watson. As I have freely admitted many times, Mycroft's powers of deduction are far superior to my own. His shortcoming stems from the fact that he lacks the initiative to follow up on his own conclusions. Mycroft simply dragged Dacres here so I could interview him, examine the ransom note, and confirm Mycroft's hypotheses."

"Which were?"

Holmes gestured to his brother, indicating that it would be best if he were to answer my question himself. With a faint but obvious trace of reluctance, Mycroft took over the conversation. "It's quite simple. Part of my job requires me to review the accounts of several secret departments. A couple of months ago, I took a look at the Ministry for the Prevention of Scandal's numbers, and it occurred to me that this wasn't just a case of profligate spending. I had a strong suspicion that someone was padding the numbers. All those millions spent covering up the filthy secrets of our politicians and titled figures! All those guineas spent when a handful of shillings would do. I knew that someone was running sticky fingers through the till. But was it a secretary, a mid-level employee, or did the rot start at the very top? I didn't have a definite answer to that, so I turned to my brother."

"I should tell you, Watson," Holmes explained, "that I have been investigating Dacres' financial institution for some weeks, and while I discovered a couple of secret accounts held by Dacres under an alias in Switzerland, I could not account for the lion's share of the money. I recently discovered, however that Dacres and both of his sons share a passion for the gaming table. Some discreet inquires prove that the family's losses over the past year have been dramatic, even crippling. Yet the family has exhibited no decline in their standard of living whatsoever. Why is this? Either the people they owe money to are remarkably forgiving, or, much more likely, they have a heretofore unknown source of income that is allowing them to cancel out their considerable debts."

"Excellent investigative work, my dear brother, but I must say that you may have missed one significant detail. While Dacres has been funneling some of his ill-gotten gains into banks overseas, he's also been smuggling a king's ransom of cash into a special, gigantic, hidden safe in the basement of his estate in Ipswich. Of course, he'd have to be very careful about drawing attention by spending it, but his embezzlement has made him one of the wealthiest men in the country. At least, he was. My men are poised to raid his home to recover the funds. A rather different approach will be used to drain his Swiss bank accounts."

As is often the case when the brothers Holmes overwhelm me with a considerable quantity of information, my head began to lose its equilibrium a bit. I still had enough lucidity to ask a question. "But if Dacres has amassed such a considerable amount of money, why would he engage in this farcical subterfuge about a kidnapping and counterfeit half-crowns?"

The brothers made eye contact, Holmes gave his elder sibling a very faint nod, and with some reluctance Mycroft answered my question. "His sons, as we mentioned, are gamblers with terrible luck. A few weeks ago the pair of them participated in a card game with the ambassador of a country that will remain nameless. They didn't just lose their shirts, they figuratively lost every stitch of clothing at Harrods as well. The debt was so massive that it would have wiped out their not-so-proud father's nest egg and would probably have necessitated the sale of the family estate to boot. Indeed, though I have no proof, I'm quite sure that the card game wasn't completely aboveboard, and that the youths were well-plied with alcohol to bet far above their station. I fully suspect that this was all a carefully orchestrated plot by the government in question to gain a sample of our imitation silver alloy."

"But now they do have it," I interjected.

"My dear Watson, please try to give me a little credit. I did not achieve my current role in the British government by being unable to anticipate oncoming threats. For months, I knew that a foreign power was after our collection of counterfeit half-crowns. So some time ago, I had the imitations replaced in order to protect the secrets of the alloy."

"So you replaced them with real half-crowns? Excellent! That means that the government's only out a hundred pounds."

"Not even that, Doctor. I am by nature a parsimonious man. I replaced the imitation half-crowns with more counterfeit half-crowns. However, this second batch were not cast with a secret alloy, but rather with plain tin. I should very much like to see the expressions on the faces of the members of the nameless foreign government's face when they learned that all they've gotten for their trouble is a few pounds of scrap metal."

This statement seemed to galvanize Dacres. "But... but... They'll think I betrayed them! They'll seek vengeance!"

"Tut, tut, sir," Holmes replied disapprovingly. "You'll be safe enough in prison."

"No!" Dacres sat bolt upright. "Here are my terms. You will allow me to keep every farthing of the money I've... accumulated over the years. I've earned it. I've kept the nation solid and respected. Then you'll set me and my family up under new identities in a comfortable estate somewhere in the colonies with a decent climate. Probably the Caribbean."

"And what makes you think that they'll comply with your ridiculous requests, you scoundrel?" I scoffed.

"Because if they don't, I've arranged for a dossier of the most humiliating secrets of some of the most powerful people in England to be released to the public! The government won't survive the scandal, and if my associate doesn't see the signal by seven o'clock tonight, he'll drop the parcel off at the rooms of a reporter I know who won't be bullied into silence."

Dacres' face flushed with triumph, only for this new confidence to fade as Mycroft's face remained impassive. Mycroft calmly removed a large blue handkerchief from his jacket pocket and waved it casually in front of the window to his left.

"What are you doing?"

"Signaling, Dacres. Surely that's obvious. Don't bother getting up. If you get up and run you'll only get caught sooner."

Moments later, three men in dark suits burst into the room. "Take him," Mycroft declared, folding up the handkerchief.

"You're making a terrible mistake! England will be doomed!" Dacres yelled as the men grabbed him and dragged him away from us.

"I doubt it." Mycroft turned to Holmes. "Will you settle the matter?"

"Of course. Watson, will you join me?"

I agreed, even though I had no idea what I was expected to do. The next thing I knew, we were riding in a carriage, heading west.

"You see, Watson, Mycroft and I anticipated his last desperate gambit. We knew he had a secret signal to tell his confederate when to release the package of damaging information.

139

Since Dacres rarely went anywhere besides his offices and his flat, it stood to reason that the signal was based at his home. My Irregulars have kept a careful eye on the place, figuring that the secret sign must be visible from the street, and within the first three days they discovered that each night, when he returns home at a quarter to seven, he hangs a small piece of stained-glass artwork in a window facing the main road. And then shortly before he retires to bed, he removes it, and repeats the process the next day. The Irregulars have been on the watch for someone who walks by every night and looks up at the window. I trust that they'll be able to help us tonight."

Holmes, as usual, was right. As soon as we stepped out of our carriage, a young street urchin hurried up to us. "You're just in time, Mr. Holmes. The fellow that we're pretty sure is our man arrived ten minutes ago. He looked up at the window and looked shocked when that piece of colored glass wasn't there. He's been standing there, leaning against that wall for ten minutes, smoking a cigarette and looking up, waiting and seeing if that stained glass appears."

"Well done, all of you! Take your positions, just in case something goes wrong." Holmes directed me to walk four paces ahead of him, and I walked right past the man with the cigarette, only to whirl around as soon as I heard Holmes' voice.

"Are you Mr. Dacres' friend?"

Upon hearing Holmes, the man dropped his cigarette and turned as if to flee, but Holmes and I both grabbed an arm and pinioned him against the wall. Holmes patted his jacket, and after a few moments extracted a very thick envelope from one pocket.

A few minutes later, Dacres' associate was in the custody of the police, and Holmes and I were riding back to turn the envelope over to Mycroft.

"I say, Holmes, who would have ever thought all those years ago that when that poor engineer came to me with his thumb severed, that it would lead to a case like this a decade later?"

Holmes shrugged and leaned back into his seat. "I dare say that Mycroft could have anticipated such a possibility. He has the sort of mind where every event, no matter how trivial, can be connected to the general health of the government. I consider myself fortunate that I can dedicate my mental powers to the investigation of crime, rather than applying them to realm of politics."

The Switched String

"There are some intriguing potential crimes in the newspaper, Holmes."

I had expected Holmes to reply with a nonplussed "*Potential crimes, Watson? What do you mean by that?*" Instead, he remained completely focused on playing his violin. I cleared my throat a couple of times, trying to catch his attention, but he continued to play a complex and fast-paced piece for the next three minutes. When he finally lowered his bow with a flourish, he turned to me and said, "Indeed, Watson. I counted no less than sixteen likely crimes that might take place in the coming week."

I had only discovered three, but I was reluctant to reveal this fact to Holmes. "There's a new exhibition of Vermeer paintings at a local gallery, which might lead to a potential theft. I see there's a report of a gang of anarchists that are targeting prominent manor houses for arson. And there's that ambassador from Eastern Europe who is making a speech tomorrow. He's considered very controversial, and there are rumors that he's been targeted for an assassination."

"Quite right, Watson. Of course, you've overlooked how a construction project might provide cover for robbing a local bank; the wedding announcement for a terminally ill duke to a woman forty years his junior– his nephew, who is currently the heir to the title, certainly has a motive to see his uncle pass before he can sire a son; a seemingly benevolent charity that on closer examination appears to be a confidence scheme..." Holmes continued for several minutes, leaving me feeling like I'd been out in the sun for far too long. No one has a better premonition of impending crime than Holmes.

Once Holmes finished his lengthy list of potential lawbreaking, there was a twinkle in his eye that forewarned me that he was about to issue a challenge that I had little chance of passing. "If you'll allow me to change the subject, Watson, did you notice anything amiss with my violin playing just now?"

I thought for a moment. "I don't believe so. You sounded just like you normally do."

"Nothing amiss or discordant?"

"I said that your playing sounded normal to me, Holmes."

"Hmm. I suppose that I have an advantage on you, as I was able to use not just my hearing abilities to identify the problem, but my powers of sight as well. Observe, Watson, the "A" string here."

"What of it?"

"Examine it, dear fellow. What differentiates it from the other strings?"

At first I saw nothing, but then Holmes tilted the violin very slightly, allowing the light to reflect off of the strings. "That "A" string… it's a slightly different color from the others, isn't it?"

"It is indeed, Watson! What else?"

I took the violin from Holmes and scrutinized it more thoroughly. "It's rather hard to tell using just my vision, but doesn't that string look a tiny bit thinner that the others?"

"Most certainly, my friend! Also—" Holmes extended a finger and tapped the string in question. "If you will use your sense of touch, you will note that it is decidedly less supple than the other strings." I ran my fingers lightly over the strings and confirmed that this was indeed the case.

"Holmes, my ears are not so trained and musical as yours are. How does the quality of this string compare to the others?"

"It is decidedly inferior. The pitch is off, and any note played in this string lacks resonance. It is a cheap string, the kind no one with any appreciation for music or pride in performance would use. Young children might use strings like this when they are learning how to play for the first time, when they need to learn technique."

"Then you would never place a string like this on your violin?"

"It would be akin to slapping Stradivarius across the face."

"Then how did it get there?"

"Ah! That is the question I've been asking myself for the last several minutes."

"What are your theories, Holmes?"

"The first question centers around opportunity. Who had the chance to defile my instrument in this manner? I know that I had nothing to do with it. The violin's strings were perfectly fine yesterday. We have had no clients visiting our rooms in the past twenty-four hours. There is only one other man with access to this violin. His motive? Perhaps he wished to play some sort of practical joke, or perhaps he sought to provide me with an unexpected and irresistible puzzle?"

There was a twinkle in Holmes' eye, but I felt no merriment whatsoever. "I can assure you that I had nothing to do with changing the string on your violin."

"Are you certain of that?"

"I am not in the habit of damaging musical instruments in my sleep, Holmes."

145

"No, you are not. I realized that you had nothing to do with this as soon as I saw your facial expressions when I queried you about the string. But if you are not responsible, then that means that someone else must have done this. So who had the opportunity? Could someone have crept into our rooms while we slept? It's possible. I didn't lock my violin away, and locks can be picked."

"It would have had to be an outsider. Mrs. Hudson would never do anything like this."

"I agree, but I think we should question her. Remember, we went out to dinner at Simpson's Divan last night. We were gone for over two hours, it's possible that someone could have crept inside without our knowledge, but that means that someone would have had to come inside without Mrs. Hudson observing him as well."

Holmes summoned Mrs. Hudson, and she confirmed his conclusion that she knew nothing about what had happened to his violin. When asked if anybody had been inside 221B while we were gone, she replied in the negative.

"At least, not as far as I know," she added. "I wasn't here all evening. Around half past seven, a neighbor down the street came to me for help. Someone had smashed two of her windows and she needed help cleaning up the shattered glass in her living room."

"How far away was this?" Holmes looked interested.

"Just three houses down, sir. Mrs. Ardor's been a friend of mine for years, but I don't think that you know her."

"Did you find any stones or bricks in the house? If I could examine them…"

"We found nothing like that, Mr. Holmes."

Disappointed, he muttered, "Perhaps they struck the windows with a cane or something like that so as to leave fewer clues behind." Raising his voice, he asked, "Can you describe Mrs. Ardor?"

"About my age, sir, though her eyesight isn't good, and her rheumatism means it's difficult for her to sweep up a mess. That's why she needed to call on me for assistance, sir. I also helped her cover up the broken windows with some cloths, as a glazier couldn't come until the morning. Luckily it was a warm night."

"Does she have any other friends nearby?"

"Not to my knowledge. She doesn't get out much, and she's on a very limited income, living off her late husband's pension. She didn't have enough to cover the cost of replacing the glass, so I had to lend her a wee bit of my housekeeping money to pay the bill."

"So if someone damaged her home, she would almost certainly come to you for assistance," Holmes mused. "When did you return?"

"Not for over an hour. Perhaps twenty minutes to nine."

"Seventy minutes. More than enough time to perform this act of vandalism."

"Not really vandalism, is it, Holmes?" I questioned. "After all, it's easily fixed."

"Yes, and once again, the question is "why?" What could be gained by this? Why go to the trouble of damaging our neighbor's home just to lure Mrs. Hudson away? If this was a practical joke, why arrange it in a way that no one could see my reaction save you, Watson?"

"It's not like you were planning to perform at the Royal Albert Hall."

"Exactly. I can see no other acts of disruption around our rooms. This is such a tiny thing…"

After a few minutes of silence, I asked, "Whatever happened to the original string?"

"An excellent question, Watson. It had no particular value. No one would have any reason to steal it."

The three of us searched our rooms for the missing string. The hunt only lasted for three minutes before Mrs. Hudson discovered the string in the wastepaper basket.

"Hmm!" Holmes studied the string, which had been coiled up into a little ring. "It's been cut. Too damaged to restring. Yet as it was left behind, then the goal was to affect the violin rather than gain access to the string itself."

"If someone had theft in mind, why not take the whole violin?" I asked. "After all, it's quite valuable, even if you did purchase it for a fraction of its value."

"Precisely." Holmes picked up his violin and examined it further. "I wondered if someone tried to hide something inside the holes, but I can see nothing, and light shaking provides no sounds. No, I do not believe that someone removed the string in order to facilitate the insertion of some unknown object into this violin. Holmes gently laid down his instrument and then began examining the lock to the door. "Hmm! There are some new scratches here—faint but clear. I think it's reasonable to conclude that someone skilled at picking locks was here. And..." He hurried downstairs and examined the front door. "Yes, there are similar marks around the keyhole here. We can now confirm that someone was here last night while we were all away, and that someone has a good deal of training in housebreaking. An amateur would have left clearer traces of his entrance, as well as of his exit when he re-locked the door, for that matter."

"Unfortunately, we know absolutely nothing about him."

"Not quite, Watson. We know that he has large, nimble hands, is probably reasonably young and healthy, is musically inclined, and is carrying a handkerchief with cream-colored smears on it."

I balked at asking the question Holmes wished me to ask, "How could you possibly know that, Holmes?" before succumbing to the inevitable and inquiring.

"Remember the original string we found in the wastepaper basket, Watson. Most likely he wrapped it around his finger several times to form the ring we found. Given the size of the circlet, he must have rather large hands. Yet they must be quick and nimble, given the dexterity needed to pick some high-quality locks and restring an instrument. Obviously no arthritis has set in yet. Additionally, he had to have smashed our neighbor's windows and hurried away sufficiently swiftly so as not to be noticed by other people on the street, again indicating a younger man in athletic condition. He was able to unstring and restring my violin without much difficulty. While the replacement string is of a markedly inferior grade, I could not have attached it to my instrument better myself. It takes practice to develop this skill, especially when one considers that under the best circumstances, one should not have to replace violin strings too frequently."

"So he's both a trained lockpicker and a violinist?"

"We can proceed under that assumption."

"And the stained handkerchief?"

"The smears are violin polish, Watson. I applied a thin coating of it before dinner last night when I had finished playing. I noticed no finger-marks or other signs of disturbance to the veneer before I began playing. Tying a string to a violin is difficult enough with bare hands, it is far more challenging when gloves are worn. The culprit almost certainly touched this instrument with bare hands, and then wiped it down, almost certainly with a handkerchief, thereby removing both any finger-marks and most of the new polish as well. I shall need to polish it again. I rather resent having my possessions handled by an intruder."

I had almost forgotten that Mrs. Hudson was still there when she asked, "Are you sure that the violin is the only item that was touched, Mr. Holmes?"

"My initial cursory examination of our rooms has revealed nothing out of order, but it's quite possible that something equally subtle has occurred." With that, the three of us began a close, detailed examination of our possessions. Mrs. Hudson carefully flipped through every book on the shelves, checking for torn-out pages or scribbled messages. I scrutinized our furniture and found nothing amiss. Holmes was the most active of all of us, darting from corner to corner, sniffing his laboratory equipment, pulling each cigar out of the coal-scuttle and examining it, rifling through his files, shaking out the curtains, and otherwise darting around with remarkable energy.

Fifteen minutes into our search, there was a knock at the front door and a young man handed Mrs. Hudson a telegram. When she tried to give it to Holmes, he tossed it onto a side table without even glancing at it, and continued to hold his pipe-tobacco up to the light, sifting it through his fingers.

Hours passed, and I eventually became convinced that we had confirmed that every carpet fiber and floor nail was exactly where it should be. Mrs. Hudson was compelled to go to bed shortly after midnight, and I reached the point of total exhaustion a bit before three in the morning. Holmes showed no signs of weariness, and continued to give our rooms the fullest possible scrutiny. He pored through his massive index, checking to see if any or his records were added to, altered, or removed. He sifted through every article of clothing he owned, including his substantial collection of disguises, examining everything minutely for added or removed buttons, items sewn into the lining, holes, or stains. All of his chemistry supplies were tested to make sure that they had not been tainted, as was his stage makeup. Even mementos from previous cases were checked from every angle under a magnifying glass to see if they had been damaged in any way. Naturally, this painstaking search took a very long time, and several hours later, when Mrs. Hudson brought in breakfast, I realized that he had not slept at all that night.

"Did you discover anything, Holmes?"

"Nothing. I had wondered if an inferior cigarette might have been slipped into a box, or if a bottle of one of my chemistry supplies had been emptied and refilled with flour, but as far as I can tell, the violin string is the only item that is amiss."

"And you're quite sure that there's no one who would perform this sort of practical joke on you?"

"In all the time that you've known me, Watson, have you ever suspected that I am the sort of person who cavorts with merry pranksters?"

"But Holmes, what possible motive could anybody have for this?"

"Are you doubting that it happened?"

"No, I know that somebody replaced your violin string. I saw the false string, the original was rolled up and deposited in the wastepaper basket. That is undeniable. It wasn't you, I had nothing to do with it, and Mrs. Hudson would never had done anything like that in a thousand years. But the chain of events, while I do not doubt it happened, still beggars belief. Think about it. Someone waits until we have left 221B. That person then breaks our neighbor's windows and runs away. The vandal knew that our neighbor would walk to 221B and ask Mrs. Hudson for help cleaning up the broken glass, knowing that she'd be gone for the better part of an hour. The culprit hides in a place where he can watch our neighbor walk to 221B and soon after Mrs. Hudson leaves, he rushes to the door and carefully unlocks the front door, being able to do so sufficiently quickly to not draw any attention."

I paused and reflected for a moment. "It is surprising that no one saw a strange man picking the lock of the front door of 221B."

"Not really. It was dark at that time, and it was a chilly night. Few people would have been idling around the street, watching the area. Additionally, I often enter and exit our home at all hours of the day and night, wearing all sorts of disguises. A strange man fumbling at the lock is not such a rare occurrence."

"Fair enough. Then the villain hurries upstairs, picks the lock to our rooms, locates your violin, removes one string, replaces it with

154

an inferior string, and hurries out of 221B, locking the doors behind him as he goes. He then disappears into the night, having achieved his only objective." After a deep breath, I concluded. "Do you agree that is an accurate summation of events, Holmes?"

He tented his fingers and leaned back in his chair. "I believe that it was accurate until your final sentence."

"Are you saying he didn't disappear into the night?" A wave of horror swept over me. "Holmes, do you believe that he's still here, hidden somewhere in the building?"

"What? No, Watson, that is not what I mean, and that is not the portion of the sentence that I found suspect. I meant the five words, "having achieved his only objective.""

"Is there something we missed?"

"The intruder did not want the string itself. That is proven by the fact that it was tossed in the wastepaper basket. In any event, the string has no intrinsic value. Just because it was used on a Stradivarius does not make it any more valuable than any ordinary fiddle string. I certainly did not plan to audition for a position in an orchestra. No public embarrassment or any direct negative consequence could come to me from this. And we have agreed that a practical joke becomes less amusing to the prankster when the person initiating the supposed humor is not there to witness the results.

Which raises one distinct possibility. The purpose of substituting a string was to generate an indirect consequence."

"But what sort of indirect consequence could result from switching a violin string?"

"What did happen, Watson?"

"We wasted a day searching our rooms."

"Precisely! From the moment I noticed how my instrument has been defiled, I have obsessed over who might have done this and what the goal of this stunt might have been. I have been focused on this string at the expense of everything else. If I am correct in my deductions, then that means that this entire charade was meant as a distraction. A bagatelle that would demand my full attention. Something that would keep me away from something more important. Like one of the potential crimes in the newspaper we discussed earlier!"

It took me a moment of reflecting, and then everything made sense. "You mean that someone was planning a major crime, became afraid that you would become involved, and created this subtle, mystifying distraction?"

"Doesn't that make perfect sense to you?"

"I cannot say that it does."

"Consider, Watson, that a clever criminal is in the process of planning a major crime. The villain in question is aware of my existence, and for reasons that I will theorize about later believes that it is probable that I will be called into the case either immediately after the crime occurs or perhaps right before it occurs in an attempt to prevent it. Do you see a flaw in my logic?"

"After all we've been through together, Holmes, you should know how unlikely such an occurrence might be."

"My blushes, Watson. Therefore, if my involvement is not wanted in this theoretical crime, then the perpetrator must find a way to prevent my investigation. Open threats would not work. Such aggression would only serve to make me more determined to insert myself into the case. If I cannot be bullied, then perhaps I can be distracted. The only way to keep me away from a very important case is to provide me with an irresistible problem. Perhaps the person in question attempted to come up with an impossible murder or some other baffling crime. Maybe this individual's powers of creativity were not up to the task, or perhaps this plotter feared that the mystery would not be interesting enough to attract me, or I might solve the case too quickly. Perhaps after much thinking, the criminal at the heart of this mystery realized that the best way to catch my attention was to personalize the problem he created for me. Instead of planning an additional complex crime solely for the purposes of distracting me, why not derail me with a simple question?

"Why would someone change out one of your violin strings?"

"Precisely. It is reminiscent of Lewis Carroll's famous riddle in *Alice's Adventures in Wonderland*: How is a raven like a writing desk?" Holmes paused for a few moments, and I pondered before admitting defeat.

"There is no answer. Carroll deliberately proposed a riddle that he didn't have a solution for. Of course, over the years readers have proposed their own solutions, such as "they both produce notes," "they both have inky quills," and my personal favorite, "Edgar Allan Poe wrote on both." But the point is that when Carroll wrote that riddle, it was designed to go unanswered. So it is with the violin string substitution. There is no rhyme or reason for the action *in itself*. It is the *consequence* of the switch that is of paramount importance. The person involved might have put pepper in my tobacco, or gold sovereigns in my dressing-gown pockets, or even left an actual wild goose in my bedroom for me to chase. The point is that I was meant to become obsessed with this ridiculous, pointless charade, and my opponent triumphed spectacularly. Full marks to him."

"But who would do such a thing? Who would not only plot a terrible crime, but go through all of this rigmarole just to prevent you from getting involved?"

"Once we find the crime, my dear fellow, we will have our answer. We have not have any potential clients knocking on our door, have we? Could the solution to this puzzle have been turned away?"

"No one has been to 221B since that boy delivered that telegram–" Scarcely had the words escaped my lips than Holmes leapt up, sprinted across the room, and retrieved the missive. "It is from a Baron Culmond, a man who has worked with my brother Mycroft on many previous occasions. It seems that he is hosting that Eastern European ambassador you mentioned yesterday. He's concerned for the diplomat's safety, and if I am correct, he has every right to be."

In less than a minute, Holmes, who was disheveled from the previous night's escapade, had thrown on a coat and had summoned a hansom cab. As we drove away from Baker Street, I asked him, "But you can't be certain that this is *the* crime you think you were distracted from, can you?"

"No, but seeing as how no one else has tried to hire me lately, and given the importance of this ambassador, it is by far the most likely option. The ambassador in question here is pivotal to resolving a trade dispute between England and his home country. If he were to die on British soil, then the negotiations would fall apart, and someone who was well-positioned in the business world could conceivably make hundreds of thousands of pounds from the resulting economic chaos."

A half-hour later, we arrived at Baron Culmond's home, and after some very terse words with the butler, the Baron met us in the hall. "Mr. Holmes. You never responded to my telegram, so I assumed that you had no interest in my worries."

"I apologize, sir. I was caught up in a very clever scheme orchestrated by the man who I believe is planning to assassinate the ambassador at any moment."

After a few words of shock and concern, the Baron led us into the ballroom where the ambassador was addressing an audience of about fifty guests. Holmes scanned the room, and after about seven seconds, he spun around and sprinted out the door. I hurried after him, but I was so far behind Holmes that I could barely hear my friend declare, "He's outside, Watson! He's in the oak tree!"

When I finally caught up with Holmes, he was crouched behind a shrub in the courtyard. He placed a finger over his lips and then pointed upwards. I could see a shadowy figure sprawled out on a very thick branch halfway up the tallest tree, pointing a rifle at the window. Holmes' eyes darted around the ground before discovering a rock the size of his fist, and upon grabbing it, he hurled it upwards at the gunman, striking him on the head. The man and his rifle hurtled to the ground with an unsettling thud.

"Is he alive, Watson?"

After a brief examination I nodded. "He's unconscious and I suspect one arm and both legs are broken, but he ought to survive."

"He shall live long enough to be tried and convicted," Holmes declared, and he was right. We summoned the authorities, who carried the gunman away on a stretcher, managing to do so without disturbing the guests inside the house.

Upon learning of our actions, the Baron and the ambassador were both effusive in their thanks. The agents of both governments decided to speed up their negotiations, and a deal was struck and signed shortly after midnight. The ambassador returned home the following day without incident.

Holmes and I returned to Baker Street as soon as the treaty was signed. "There's just one unanswered question, Holmes."

"Oh? What's that?"

"Who was behind all of this? Who not only planned the death of the ambassador in order to profit from the resulting chaos, but who knew that you would be involved, and that you would be distracted by a little adjustment to your violin? Who would break our neighbor's windows, knowing that Mrs. Hudson would be called away to help?"

Holmes sighed. "You ought to know the answer to that, Watson. Only one criminal in all of England knows my character so well, realizes the danger I pose to him, and could position himself to turn international upheaval into a small fortune. I suppose I should be flattered that he only sought to distract me instead of killing me. I have no strength to discuss my nemesis now, as I am spent. I have not slept in over forty hours. If you will excuse me, my good fellow…"

And with that, Holmes staggered into his bedroom for some well-deserved rest.

The Bitter Gravestones

Sherlock Holmes was not having a happy Christmas. He was tired, a little bitter, and would much rather have been back with his honeybees.

He had not wanted to spend the holiday at an isolated manor house in the countryside, but his brother Mycroft had requested that he make the visit and protect the nation's interests at a top-secret conference there. Although I cannot go into details as the event is still a state secret, by the morning of the twenty-fourth of December the matters being decided were satisfactorily resolved and the assorted diplomats had left hurriedly in order make their way home in time for the holiday. Holmes was under orders to remain at the manor house until Boxing Day to tie up loose ends and await the arrival of a government agent for further instructions.

Holmes had invited me along, privately warning me that my presence was necessary to preserve his sanity. He had previously met the Blurdells, the family who owned the manor, and they were not the sort of people who Holmes would willingly spend time with given the option. Once Holmes had done his duty to King and Country and sent the last of the diplomats on his way, Holmes retreated to his room and asked that his meals be delivered to him on a tray.

"Surely, Holmes, you don't intend to spend the entirety of Christmas in your room? I'm aware that you aren't feeling particularly warm towards the Blurdells, which, having gotten to know most of them over the last two days, I can rather understand. But Christmas is Christmas, and wouldn't you rather share your goose and pudding with other people?"

The glare on Holmes' face was far more chilling than the icy winds whipping around the mansion. "I can assure you, Watson, that having devoted all of my energies to maintaining peace on earth, I now no longer have the strength to muster any goodwill to all men. I have done my part to prevent the recurrence of those horrors that plagued our continent for four long and violent years recently. I do not deserve the torment of having to pull Christmas crackers with Lord Derek Blurdell or listen to Horace Blurdell's tired jokes as he drains a decanter of port. I have a quiet room, a couple of books, and enough paper and writing equipment to begin work on the monograph I have been planning for some time. Should for some reason I desire conversation, I can always speak to you, dear fellow. Otherwise, I shall be perfectly happy being left to my own devices."

I chose not to argue further with Holmes, as in my heart I knew he was completely correct. For most people, any company is better than none at Christmas. Not so for Holmes.

We spoke little over the next few minutes, and I was about to return to my room and take a little nap before dinner when there was a knock at the door. Before Holmes could utter a response, a thirteen-year-old boy hurried into the room and shut the door behind him. It was Duncan Blurdell, the only surviving son of Lord Derek Blurdell, his older brothers having perished in the war. "Mr. Holmes? Doctor Watson?"

"Yes, Duncan? What is it?" I asked.

"I need to talk to you about the gravestones."

"What's wrong with them?" Holmes asked, not bothering to hide the asperity in his voice.

"They're so *bitter*, sir. It doesn't make sense."

"How can a gravestone be bitter?"

"It's what's inscribed on them, Mr. Holmes. Six relatives I've never met or even heard of. They all died on Christmas, one a year for the past six years. And what's written on the gravestones is truly vile, sir. Not Christian at all. But if someone's died every Christmas for over half a decade, well, what if the pattern holds and someone else dies tomorrow? I don't know for sure, but it can't be a coincidence that six members of the family died on that date so regularly, sir. If we could find out what's going on, maybe we could prevent tomorrow's death, sir."

Holmes' facial expression and posture altered completely, and I noticed that familiar spark of interest that he gets whenever he decides that a problem is worthy of his skills. "Can you lead us to the gravestones?"

"Yes, sir. They're not far from the house."

"Get your coat, Watson, and meet us outside my door. I very much want to see these gravestones."

As I rummaged through the hall closet for my coat, I felt my eyes water from the abundance of pine. Multiple large trees had been installed in the entryway, and evergreen boughs festooned the archways. A few minutes later, we were walking along a lightly trampled pathway in the dead grass, wrapping our coats tightly around us to protect ourselves from the blustery wind. "How long have you been aware of these gravestones, Duncan?" Holmes asked.

"I just discovered them twenty minutes ago, sir. I don't like to visit the graveyard, it's not a pleasant place. But I was playing with my dog, Rex. He's a spaniel. We were playing near the edge of the woods, about a quarter-mile south of the family cemetery, and all of a sudden he started running off. Well, I followed him, and when I got there Rex was sniffing around these six gravestones in the corner. I tried to shoo him away, but he started howling, and he drew my attention to what was written on them, sir. Gave me the chills, it did. That's why I came to you, thinking you might be able to make sense of it all."

The wind grew steadily stronger as we made our way to the cemetery. It was a small square of land surrounded on three sides by the woods, and completely enclosed by an iron fence. Unlike every other portion of the estate, there were no Christmas decorations to be found around the graveyard. We pushed through the unlocked gate. There were about seventy gravestones scattered around the graveyard in no apparent order. Most of them were large, ornate slabs of shining marble. Duncan led us towards the back of the area, where six gravestones stood far apart from the nearest markers.

The first four gravestones in the line were small pieces of cheap tan rock, each about a foot tall. The first gravestone read:

Elspeth Blurdell Hill

.June 3 1881 – December 25 1919

She Will Not Be Mourned

"Who would write that on a gravestone?" I asked.

"Wait until you see the others," Duncan informed me.

The words on the second gravestone were:

John Blurdell

March 3 1884 – December 26 1920

Good riddance to bad rubbish

I was flabbergasted.   Holmes looked fascinated.   As we moved to the third gravestone, we read the words:

Alicia Blurdell White

December 15 1900 – December 25 1921

Liar

Adulteress

Murderess

"Murderess? Who is she supposed to have killed?"

"We shall have to look into that, Watson."

The fourth grave was no less malicious or baffling.

Gregory Blurdell

August 11 1847 – December 25 1922

S.I.T.

Suffer In Torment

The fifth gravestone was a bit larger than the first four, and was made of much nicer material.

Thomas Blurdell

February 27 1898 – December 25 1923

If only he had been stillborn, the world would have been a happier place.

"What a heartless thing to write!"

"Possibly, Watson. Observe this sixth gravestone."

The sixth gravestone was by far the largest and most ornate. It was the only one to resemble the other prominent markers in the cemetery. This one actually had a poem inscribed on it:

Daniel Blurdell

January 2 1897 – December 25 1924

Here rots the corpse of Dan Blurdell

The worst sinner since Adam fell

His breath gave off a loathsome smell

If he had virtues none could tell

Not once in life did he mean well

We hope the bastard roasts in hell

"How appalling!" I blurted out uncontrollably.

"Not appalling, Watson, so much as intriguing. The odds of six people in the same family dying on Christmas over the course of six consecutive years defies the odds."

"Why would someone carve such sentiments on a gravestone, where anybody can see it?"

"Not anybody, Watson. Remember, this is a private graveyard in the middle of the countryside. The only people likely to ever see this are the Blurdell family and their servants."

"And not many of either group you mention, Mr. Holmes," Duncan chimed in, "Most of the family and servants don't much like to spend time in the graveyard. It's an unsettling place, sir. Every now and then someone comes in on an anniversary or something, but more often than not we never visit. There's a gardener who comes in once in a while to tidy up everything, but not many other people."

"Interesting. When was the last time you were in here before today, Duncan?"

"For my brothers' joint funeral back in 1919. They were all killed in the war, but we didn't get their bodies back until long after all the battles had ended. I've been at school when all of the other family members' funerals were held." Duncan pointed across the graveyard at four headstones, each with a stone bust on the top. "They all died during the last six months of fighting, sir. If the war

171

had just ended a couple of months earlier, maybe a couple of my brothers could've made it home."

"I'm so sorry, Duncan."

"It isn't your fault, Mr. Holmes. I know I should come here more often, but, well, I just don't like it here. I'm away at school most of the time anyway. I didn't know them all that well because they were so much older than I was, but that didn't mean we weren't close, sir."

"You do not have to explain yourself." Holmes started walking around the other gravestones. "There seems to be a clear disparity in these monuments to the dead. The holders of the earldom, those who died in battle... most of them receive enormous headstones, often with some sort of tribute inscribed on it. Others, mainly women and those who died young, get smaller headstones, with much simpler inscriptions, just the names and dates. Still, the rest of these are made out of high-quality material, unlike those four stones there, which might crumble over a relatively short period of time when exposed to the elements. You can see the first of the bitter gravestones has already developed the first hints of a crack. It won't last another decade. So the point arises– someone loathed these people enough that they were willing to carve their venom onto a slab of rock, but they didn't care enough to buy sufficiently durable material so that their rancor would last throughout the ages."

"And why are the last two headstones nicer than the others?" I wondered. "Do you think that whoever purchased them loathed the deceased, but thought that they deserved a lasting monument to their awfulness?"

"My father would have bought those headstones," Duncan noted. "As the head of the family, it's his job to handle all of the major purchases."

"Duncan, you understand that I have to ask these questions, even if they are rather personal," Holmes explained. "Are there financial reasons why your father might have been compelled to scrimp a lot on those headstones?"

"Not really, sir. He certainly spared no expense for my brothers' graves. He's complained about the cost of my school fees, but he's never been unable to pay them. The staff doesn't seem to be any smaller than it was in the past. I haven't noticed any paintings missing from the walls, and as far as I can tell my mother still has all of her jewels. Actually, my father's bought her an enormous diamond necklace for Christmas this year, but please don't tell her and spoil the surprise until tomorrow."

"I see. What do you know about the six people in the graves?"

"Nothing, Mr. Holmes."

"Surely you must have heard something about them?"

"Well, I can't be sure, because when my grandfather was alive before the war, he was always telling long and rambling stories about the family, but I never really listened, so it's certainly possible that he mentioned them at some point but they didn't stay in my mind."

"Did you ever meet any of them?"

"No, sir, not as far as I can remember, but there are a great many family members that I've never seen. You see, a lot of my relatives have led rather... *scandalous* lives. Plenty of them have run off with lovers, some have wasted massive amounts of money gambling. and there's no shortage of cousins who bear the family name, but whose parents were never married. There's probably dozens of relatives who are considered embarrassments. I suppose the official family policy is that if someone's not considered sufficiently respectable, they are *persona non grata*. Their names are never mentioned, there are no pictures of them anywhere, and they're never invited to the manor house. Every now and then the family lawyers may send them some money, but I don't know why. Maybe they've been very good, or maybe they're in terrible trouble, or perhaps they're threatening to make an embarrassing scene and my father bribes them to mind their manners." Duncan shuddered. "We're a rather idiosyncratic family."

Holmes shrugged. "You're really not that different from other wealthy and prominent families."

"Do you know any other families who write messages like this on gravestones?"

"No. Which makes this situation all the more intriguing." After a moment's pause, Holmes asked, "How many of these estranged relatives have been buried in the family plot?"

"As far as I can tell, none of them, at least since I was born. I've looked around, and I recognize the names of everyone who's died in my lifetime." Duncan gestured. "I see my grandparents and some great-aunts and uncles, and of course my brothers. I never met my great-aunt Cicely, who lived in Paris since she was twenty-one, but she was mentioned all the time before she died four years ago. Our cousin Gerald, who comes from the branch of the family with no money of their own, he works in the family archives and traces the family genealogy. My parents often sit me next to him at family dinners, possibly because no one else wants to listen to him talking about our ancestors and distant relatives. Just last night at dinner, he was talking about someone rather high up on our family tree who fought at the Battle of Bosworth Field. I don't remember what side that person was on, though."

"Hmm. Let's take another look at the gravestones." Holmes walked back to the start of the line of markers. "Elspeth Blurdell Hill. Indicating that she was married, or possibly was the daughter of a Blurdell daughter who married a Hill and wanted to make sure the Blurdell name was not lost. A little under forty. Can you think of any other relatives named "Ellie" or "Ella" or any other potential derivatives?"

"No, sir. I have a distant cousin named Eleanor, but she's only six or so."

"Very well. Five words in the epitaph. "She Will Not Be Mourned." Simple, terse, but vague. That is notable, especially when paired with some of the other headstones."

I was a bit confused. "What do you mean, Holmes?"

"Simply put, writing an angry epitaph on a gravestone is the ultimate way of having the last word in an argument. It's a means of shaming the person you held a grudge against long after death. The deceased can't respond. So why not be more specific? Why won't she be mourned? What did she do wrong? We can't tell from this gravestone, only that no one is going to miss her. But that leads to other deductions. If she was married, then it assumes that her husband is either deceased or than they were not on warm terms. If she had children, something so terrible must have happened that the maternal bond was absolutely severed. Surely what she did would have to be utterly horrific if it were to cut her connection with her own parents, unless of course they were already dead."

"That seems reasonable, Holmes."

"But that ignores a major question. What is she doing here? Why is she buried here? Duncan, since you have no knowledge of her, can she really be that close of a relative? No matter how estranged she was from her family, they allowed her to be buried here. And if she wasn't that close to the Lord Derek Blurdell, why would he have so much rancor towards her that he would carve those words on her gravestone?"

"Perhaps whatever the reasons for that estrangement, Lord Blurdell didn't want to expose the family to scandal?"

"Then why put those words on the headstone at all, Watson? If he wanted to hush up the scandal, all he needed to do was put her name and the relevant dates on the stone. Nothing more. A comment like this is enough to raise eyebrows. If he had those words carved on the headstone, he must have wanted someone to see them. He clearly didn't think enough of Mrs. Elspeth to spend much money on a headstone, yet he willingly paid the engraver extra money to carve that vicious comment. Why pay for a that, and use a low-quality stone that is likely to crumble within a decade? I repeat, if someone wanted to immortalize their bitterness in stone, why not spend a little extra money to make the anger last? It's contradictory, Watson."

"True." After listening to Holmes' reasoning, I was feeling a little dizzy.

"The same principle applies to the grave of John Blurdell. Once again, Duncan, you know nothing of him?"

"I don't believe so, Mr. Holmes. I know an uncle and a couple of cousins named John, but they're all alive and on good terms with the rest of the family."

"I see. The same questions from the first gravestone apply here. The inscription is cutting, cold, and completely devoid of context. The grave of Alicia Blurdell White is far more promising. Only twenty-one years old. Hmm! A liar? That can be said for most of us. Adulteress? That implies that she was married to a Mr. White, but why would Mr. White want to advertise the fact that he was cuckolded? Why would anyone else want to advertise that fact in such a manner? And "Murderess?" Who did she kill?"

"Perhaps she killed her husband so she could marry her lover, Mr. Holmes. Or maybe she killed her lover to prevent a scandal," Duncan theorized.

"Possibly, possibly. But why advertise this? In any event, I am extremely well-informed as to the crime news in this country. I am aware of every person who met a sticky end on the gallows over the past few decades. And I am quite certain that Mrs. White's name is not on that list. Therefore, she was not hanged. Of course, she might have been tried and executed overseas, but would they have shipped the body back here? I suppose that could be true. Might she have committed suicide, or met a violent end at the hands of someone avenging the victim? Twenty-one is a young age to die of natural causes, though of course it happens all the time. And how are we to know that she was really guilty of murder? I know of no trial. It's possible that this woman was falsely accused."

"Not just of murder, but of adultery as well," I mused.

"Very true, Watson. We have to bear in mind that these gravestones may not be telling us the absolute truth. It's quite possible that they're only telling one side of the story. Or rather, one side of six stories." Holmes cleared his throat. "And now, we need to address a critical issue, the dates on the tombstones. Not the birthdates, though there may be some points of importance there that might be unearthed through further study. It's the death dates."

Duncan nodded. "I was wondering that myself, sir. How come all of them died on Christmas? If this happened once, it's perfectly understandable, and twice is a coincidence, but it can happen. But six deaths, all on Christmas? It just seems to be beyond the realm of possibility."

"Left to pure chance, then I agree with you, Duncan. However, there's also the possibility of design, as well."

"You mean they were murdered, Mr. Holmes? All on Christmas?"

"That is one of multiple possibilities. It is also perfectly conceivable that the death dates are a fabrication made out of convenience."

"What do you mean, Holmes?"

"Sometimes when it's not clear when people have died, a date is picked somewhat randomly. This happened a lot during the war. Often for various reasons, it could not be determined exactly when a person was killed. Perhaps it was in the middle of a late-night skirmish and no one knew whether the fatal bullet was fired before or after midnight. Maybe a solider was shot while travelling through the countryside and his body was not discovered by his comrades until a week later. Often, just to get the necessary paperwork out of the way, one date would be selected because it was just as good as another."

"That happened with two of my brothers," Duncan nodded. "They were in the Asian-Pacific theatre of the war, and one got captured and the other got separated from the others in an attack. When their bodies were found, no one knew when they'd died, so in both cases the authorities just went with the date the corpse was discovered. Luckily the legal question worked out without much confusion."

"What legal question?" I asked.

"Their wills, sir. My brother Timmy divided his possessions amongst his four brothers, and my brother Arthur said that his gold watch went to Timmy unless Timmy predeceased him, in which case the watch would go to his wife– Arthur's wife, I mean. Widow, now. Well, even though officially Arthur was supposed to have died a couple of days before Timmy, the bodies had clearly been dead long before they were found, so we just don't know for certain who died first. If Arthur died first, Timmy would get the watch, and since Timmy and my other brothers are dead, the watch would go to me. But if Timmy died first, Arthur's widow got the watch. It could've led to a big court battle if a lot of money had been involved, but Arthur's widow, she's a nice lady, and she told me she wanted me to have the watch." Duncan pulled a pocket watch from his jacket. "I'd much rather have my brothers back, though. Arthur's widow got married again a couple years ago, and just had a baby girl. That's nice for her." He replaced the watch and turned away. I suspect a tear was forming in his eye and he didn't want us to see.

181

I believe that Holmes wanted to change the topic of conversation in order to provide young Duncan with some time to compose himself. "The remaining graves do not provide us with much additional information. "Suffer in torment?" A particularly piercing emotion, telling us exactly where whoever requested that epitaph believed Mr. Gregory's soul is now. What did he do that led the person who ordered the gravestone to come to such a conclusion?"

"My father must have ordered those words," Duncan noted. "No one else would have done that or allowed such a thing to be inscribed without his approval."

"Hmm, yes. No point in trying to theorize was Mr. Gregory might have done. Not enough evidence to draw any sort of conclusion. But what of your father, Duncan? Is he the sort of man to hold a powerful, burning grudge, so much so that he would flaunt the rules of decorum and the custom of never speaking ill of the dead?"

"No, sir, not at all. He's a most restrained man. He never has been much of one for showing emotion. That's why I can't explain this at all. It makes no sense whatsoever. He's a fierce believer in keeping family secrets away from outsiders. When his sister's daughter got– well, I mustn't say, sirs. You understand the need to keep things private." We did. "He'd never order grave markers like this. It's completely out of character."

"As you noted, this is a fairly private place," I noted. "It's not like your standard church graveyard where any Tom, Dick, or Harry can walk in off the street and start scrutinizing the gravestones. And I don't think that most of your guests will ask to see this portion of the grounds."

"True enough," Holmes conceded, "But all it takes is one person to wander in here and start asking questions. In any event, there are plenty of options that could retain privacy. If one's malice towards a deceased person was so violent that they wanted to carve out a final parting shot upon a tombstone, why not have the body cremated and have the attacking words inscribed upon an urn? An urn could be hidden in a far more private place, even indoors, and since expenses were clearly spared in the first four cases, why not save even more money by choosing cremation over burial? If money was no object, why not build a crypt and keep the bitterness sagely locked inside solid walls?"

Neither I nor Duncan had any response to this, so Holmes continued. "Here is where the situation becomes even more perplexing. These last two headstones are far larger and of much better quality than the first four. The fifth headstone is of a size usually dedicated to the maiden aunts of the family, whereas the sixth headstone is almost the same size as one of your brother's markers, though without the bust atop it. Not cheap. An insult carved upon an obelisk like these will last for decades, perhaps centuries. One more point I forgot to mention about the four smaller stones. You can tell from the dead plant matter surrounding them that the grass has been allowed to cover them during the warmer months. So the groundskeeper has almost certainly been specifically ordered not to tend to those graves, which means for much of the year, the inscriptions would be unreadable. Why go through all the trouble of putting those comments upon the headstones, only to neglect the tending, meaning that the comments are only readable in the winter? Most perplexing."

Holmes coughed and adjusted his coat. "Moving on. The fifth stone's inscription is filled with loathing but is low on specifics. What did the deceased do to warrant such antipathy? It does not say. Perhaps the reference to his being "stillborn" means that he was a nasty piece of work ever since he was a child, but there is insufficient evidence to draw a solid conclusion. Hem! The final inscription is the longest and the most intriguing of all. A bit of doggerel devoted to telling the world what a rotter Dan Blurdell was. You know nothing of him either, Duncan?"

"Not a thing, Mr. Holmes."

"Hmm. Interesting. If a man is referred to as a "sinner," it's most probable that he was given to various forms of dissipation. Women? Alcohol? Gambling? All of the above? Prone to violence?

Halitosis is unpleasant, but not necessarily an indicator of poor moral character. The previous headstone, "Suffer in torment" also expressed a desire for the resident of this grave to reside in the depths of Hades. And to refer to him as the "worst sinner" is perplexing. Surely the worst sinners are the murderers, but if he had killed someone, why not mention it? Recall Alicia Blurdell White's gravestone. If she was identified as a killer, why not Daniel? Therefore, whatever his crimes, Daniel probably never took another human being's life, at least as far as the author of this inscription knew." Holmes paused. "Is your father of a poetic disposition, Duncan?"

"No, sir. He hates poetry. Mother loves it, though. She's always writing poems for our Christmas cards–" Duncan drew in his breath so hard he whistled. "I just realized, sir. My father might not have been able to have bought the gravestone last year."

"Why not?"

"Family business, sir. He was called away to Canada in late November. He didn't get back until well after Twelfth Night."

"Then perhaps your mother ordered the stone and wrote the inscription herself. It seems that your parents share antipathy towards these people." Holmes took a step forward and slapped a hand against the sixth headstone. "No, it won't do. It won't do at all. It doesn't make sense." He stooped down, withdrew a folding knife from his pocket, and began digging in the dirt in front of the sixth gravestone. After carving out a little cone, he eased it out and studied it. "Just as I suspected. Observe, Watson. The ground's hard-packed, some layering is clear. I highly doubt that someone actually dug up the ground here a year ago in order to bury a coffin."

"But if no one's buried here…"

"Then perhaps the other five graves are empty as well." I did not care for the gleam that appeared in Holmes' eyes as he spoke these words. "Duncan, do you know where we can find ourselves a shovel?"

"Holmes, you can't! It's indecent!" A memory flashed through my mind. "And probably illegal, too. Remember Mr. Frankland's comments during the Baskerville case? How it's against the law to disinter a corpse without the permission of the next of kin?"

"I'm a member of the family, aren't I?" Duncan observed. "If I say it's all right, that might take care of any legal issues, couldn't it?"

I was torn between feeling aghast and thwarted, and admiring Duncan for making a clever point.

Holmes allowed himself a little chuckle. "I dare say we should be able to make a compelling defense should the matter ever come into court, yet at this stage of my life I feel the desire to spend as little of it in a courtroom as possible. In any event, at my age I should avoid the heavy manual labor of digging a minimum of six feet into the ground. No, upon further reflection I shall not seek out the use of a shovel."

"I'm delighted to hear that, Holmes."

"I am, however, in need of a bit of exercise. Would the two of you care to join me for a brisk stroll into town? I believe the village is just over half a mile down the road."

As we walked away from the graves, I asked Holmes, "What exactly is your destination in the village, Holmes?"

"The local monumental mason, Watson. The person who designs and carves the gravestones. I noticed his shop next door to the undertaker's a few days ago, although I believe he self-styles as a "memorialist."" Holmes froze and turned around. "Just a moment. There's one further point that I observed earlier but never got around to mentioning." He pointed at the headstones. "Take a closer look at the lettering on the markers. Compare the first four to the most recent two. Pay particular attention to the letters "J" and "L" and some of the others."

Duncan's eyes were much younger and sharper than mine. "The lettering doesn't match, sir! The person who carved the first four tombstones, the ones on the poor-grade rock, he's clearly a different person from the one who covered the other two stones. And… Duncan ran around the graveyard, peering at some of the more recent headstones. "Whoever did the last two stones also did my brother's grave markers, as well as some other relatives who died over the past decade!"

"Indeed. I would very much like a word with our village memorialist."

Fifteen minutes later, we reached the village, and it looked as if everybody who lived there was filled with the Christmas spirit. Mistletoe dangled over many doorways, lit candles stood in most of the windows, and paper daisy chains were festooned everywhere. A quartet of carolers were strolling down the street singing "God Rest Ye Merry Gentlemen," and a man on one corner was selling freshly roasted chestnuts from a little cart. I purchased a small bag and shared them with Duncan. Holmes declined my offer.

Eventually, we reached the memorialist's shop, one of the few stores in the village that was not decorated for the season, which made sense given the somber nature of the business. Holmes tapped on the door. Louder knocks produced no answer, but when Holmes tried the knob, the door swung open.

"Are you sure you should be entering?" I asked as Holmes strode inside the shop.

"There is no "Closed" sign, and if he didn't want people walking in, he ought to have locked his door," Holmes replied. A moment later the three of us were wandering around the shop. Holmes pushed through a second door and found himself inside the memorialist's workroom. "Well, well, well. Watson, Duncan. Come here and take a look at this fascinating discovery, please."

We followed him into the workroom, where a substantial obelisk stood in the center of the room. Traces of stone dust were strewn all over the floor. The room was rather dark, so Holmes struck a match and held it to the marker so we could read it.

Nancy Blurdell Jones

May 5 1901 – December 25 1925

The epitaph was in huge letters that filled the rest of the stone.

THE WORLD IS A BETTER PLACE WITHOUT HER

Holmes chuckled, and I turned to him. "Do you find this kind of bitterness funny?"

"I am in awe of this memorialists' powers, Watson. Not only is he a skilled craftsman who knows how to neatly carve words into stone, but he is also a psychic. How on earth does he know that Mrs. Jones will die tomorrow?"

I had a few seconds to reexamine the stone before Holmes' match burned down to his fingertips. "You're right! How on earth could he know when she'll be passing away? Even the best doctors wouldn't dare to predict when a terminally ill person will die more than a day or two before it happens. People have an amazing ability to linger longer than we'd expect– and sometimes they die much quicker then we think. Is she planning to commit suicide on Christmas? Or is someone planning to murder her?"

Though the light was dim, I could still see Holmes shaking his head. "No, Watson. I don't think that anyone can possibly kill Mrs. Jones. She can never be murdered, nor can she commit suicide."

"Why not?"

"Because she never existed."

"I think you're right, Mr. Holmes," Duncan replied. "When I was little, all the young relatives came to the house several times a year. Even the children of relatives who were estranged from the family came, because the children weren't held responsible for what their parents did. But I never met a cousin named Nancy."

"And I'm quite willing to wager every bee in my hives that all six of the names on the other remarkable gravestones are similarly fictional."

"I believe you've got it, Mr. Holmes"

I was utterly flummoxed. "But why? Why go through all of this absurd rigmarole? Why carve out such vile hatred onto six tombstones–"

"Seven, Watson, including this one."

"Seven tombstones, all for seven supposedly hated relatives who never existed? What could possibly be the point? Is this all some sort of dark practical joke?"

"I am reluctant to cast aspersions upon Duncan's parents in front of him, but I believe that his father and mother have a fairly reasonable motive for their actions."

"His parents?" I realized the truth of this observation as the words left my mouth. "Of course. His father bought all the headstones, except for last year's, when his mother had to handle the transaction."

"And the poem on the sixth one, sir. The meter. The rhyming. It's exactly the sort of thing mother would write. It sounds exactly like one of her Christmas card poems, only with much more negative sentiments. I'm sure it's her work."

"I would not be surprised if other members of the family were aware of what is going on here."

"But what is happening, Holmes?"

"Unfortunately, I still do not have enough facts to draw a reasonable–"

He stopped at the sound of a door shutting. Wordlessly, he motioned us into a corner, and the three of us hid as best we could in the shadow of a tall shelf. A moment later a man and a woman entered the workroom.

"He's probably at the tavern drinking. He'll probably have to spend all of Christmas sleeping it off," the man grumbled.

"Well, he can wait for his money. While we're here, we might as well take a look at his work," the woman replied.

Holmes stepped forward. "Do you often come here on Christmas Eve, Lord and Lady Blurdell?"

Even in the weak light, the surprise and embarrassment on their faces was clear. Lady Blurdell was the first to regain her composure. "Mr. Holmes. Dr. Watson. Duncan. I'm rather surprised to see you here."

"That is understandable, Lady Blurdell. Please accept my condolences on your relative's passing, which will apparently happen tomorrow. Very sad. I must say that I admire your efficiency on ordering the headstone. But please, if you will excuse my overwhelming curiosity, what exactly did Nancy do to make your believe that the world is better off without her?"

Lady Blurdell rallied, and responded to Holmes' question with frigid hauteur. "I consider that a most improper question, Mr. Holmes."

"With all due respect, Lady Blurdell, you do not. In fact, you are anxious to know how I came to ask that question in the first place. A display of false indignation might work on many gentlemen, but quite frankly putting on airs of being insulted has no effect on me whatsoever. You make cast whatever aspersions you like about me based on my words. I can assure you that I am not moved one tiny bit."

Holmes' comments had a remarkable effect on Lady Blurdell. It was rather like watching a balloon deflate in a few short seconds. Lord Blurdell had the appearance of a schoolboy who had just gotten caught in a bit of mischief. "Perhaps we can work out some sort of deal, Mr. Holmes," Lord Blurdell murmured.

"Much wealthier men than you have tried to bribe me, sir, and far more powerful men have tried to threaten me. The thing you can give me now that I most desire is information. I want to know exactly what is going on with this little charade."

Lord Blurdell appeared to have no more strength left in him than his wife. "Please, not here. Anyway, how much do you know and how much have you guessed?"

"I shall recount the events of the last hour to you on the ride back to your estate. Once there, I expect you to answer all of my questions fully."

Lord and Lady Blurdell were both very quiet as Holmes informed them of everything that had happened since Duncan had come to us. Once we arrived at the manor house, the tension was cut a bit by the wonderful smell of roasting goose and cakes baking in the oven. The Blurdells led us into the library and locked the door securely.

"Would you care for a drink, Mr. Holmes?" Lord Blurdell asked.

"No, just information." Holmes caught my eye and read my thoughts. "Watson will take something, though. A whiskey, dear fellow?"

I agreed, and Lord Blurdell poured me a whiskey and soda, and prepared a particularly strong one for himself. The glass was nearly filled with whiskey, and there could not have been more than a teaspoonful of soda-water mixed in with it. Lady Blurdell took a small tumbler of brandy, and Duncan had a glass of plain soda-water. Lord Blurdell swallowed his drink in two gulps, and poured himself another of equal strength. Holmes took the glass from him and set it aside.

"I need you to be in a fit condition to answer my questions, sir. Now, you can start by confirming my suspicions. There are no bodies buried in those six graves, are there?"

Lord Blurdell shook his head. "No."

"And the names on the gravestones. They never existed, did they?"

This question caused Lord Blurdell to look up at us with a surprised expression. "Oh, no. They were all real. They just didn't live for very long. Over the years, there have been many Blurdells who died in infancy. The seven names we've used so far, they all passed away within a few days of being born. Most were born premature. It helped to have genuine birth certificates, though."

"I see. That makes a great deal of sense. The married names of the women were pure fictions, of course. Hill. White. Jones. You picked the most common names possible just to make it harder to track down their husbands if anyone was so inclined."

"Correct. We could have left them unmarried, I suppose, but... we thought that it might help to pair them up with wealthy husbands."

"In order to explain your inheritances, I suppose."

Lord Blurdell's face paled. "You guessed?"

"I did. Thank you for confirming my suspicions. At this time, many members of the landed aristocracy are pinching pennies. Many of them are suffering financially due to increased taxation, death duties, and all sorts of unwanted expenditures. You are doing quite well for yourselves. I see no spaces on the walls where priceless portraits have been sold off, no gaps on the shelves for missing antiques, no housing developments where large tracts of land have been put on the auction-block. Your staff is massive, your wines top-notch, and I have been informed by a reliable source that your Christmas present for your wife is absolutely extravagant. What does this mean? You are enjoying an impressive source of income, something that's allowing you to indulge in extravagances. I know that your home is used by the British government to entertain foreign dignitaries on a near-monthly basis. I believe you get some recompense for your hosting duties, but just enough to cover expenses. Unless, of course, you are finding ways to pad the bills?"

A very ugly smile passed over Lord Blurdell's face. "Blackmail, Mr. Holmes. It's been easy to stand aside and watch these powerful politicians lounge about our homes like they own the place. I've seen who they smuggle in at night, I know what substances they consume, and I hear them talk amongst themselves about how they've been skimming off the top of the various public funds at their disposal. Oh yes, Mr. Holmes. Our Parliament and Foreign Office are full of depraved and venal men. They do not govern our nation wisely. They simply live in the pursuit of pleasure, filling their pockets and living better than the King at the nation's expense."

"And you are particularly offended by this," Holmes replied. It was a statement, not a question.

"Those wretched degenerates killed nearly all of my sons!" Lady Blurdell finally broke her silence. She was a small woman, fragile in build, and the violence that coursed through her body gave the impression that the force of her rage would tear her to pieces. "My four eldest boys all died in the war, Mr. Holmes. And for what?

197

Is the world any better than it was in 1913, before the conflict started? Are the nations of the world wiser and more humane? Did all those untold numbers of people make the ultimate sacrifice for the greater good? If they did, Mr. Holmes, I can't see it! And who started the war? It was foolish, short-sighted, arrogant, pompous politicians like the ones who tell us they're commandeering our home at a moment's notice, and expect oysters and lobsters and thick steaks and the finest wines and liquor. We must find African violets for the Swedish ambassador's room, they're his favorite. It doesn't matter that it's January, we need to find some strawberries for the Spanish consul. This mattress won't do for the Italian delegate's wife. Get another of the finest goose down right away. And speaking of the beds! They turn our home into a den of iniquity that Caligula himself would be ashamed to enter! These are the men who govern the nation, Mr. Holmes. These aren't statesmen, they're confidence tricksters who are addicted to power and dissipation. They ran us straight into four years of hell on earth, and at the end of it, when we were burying caskets full of our children and wondering if we'd ever be able to stop crying, these men made glorious speeches about how they were going to keep the world safe and secure, and while they bankrupted our friends with new taxes, they used those funds for their own endless revelry. Well, can you really blame us, Mr. Holmes? We had the chance. We waited until they made their way back to their homes. I won't tell you who we recruited, but we managed to blackmail them in a way that they never suspected we were involved. So several years ago, we started, and soon we collected a small fortune from them. But then we were stuck with a problem."

As Lady Blurdell seemed reluctant to continue, Holmes prompted her. "How to explain the money? You needed to spend it. And so, like the American criminals who buy small legitimate businesses in order to turn their ill-gotten gains into income they could pay their debts with and put in the bank, you needed a seemingly respectable avenue as a cover for your financial chicanery. It is a lot easier for a gangster from Chicago to buy a laundry and pretend to profit handsomely from it than it is for a British aristocrat to run a business. So how to account for the funds? You claimed to inherit them."

"I shan't give you the names of the people who helped us!" Lord Blurdell's voice showed defiance for the first time. "I won't get these decent people in trouble. They understood. They'd lost children of their own, they knew we were just getting our own back, and we paid them well to compensate them for the terrible suffering they endured. But you're right. At the end of the year, we totaled up all the money we'd collected over the past twelve months, and claimed that a long-estranged relative left us everything. To fund the maintenance of the family home– we figured that they might not have cared for us, but they had loyalty towards the house and grounds. The people who might have investigated were paid off, and after all of our expenses and dispensations, we were still enjoying a hefty profit."

"Yes, we paid a small fortune in death duties, but it was all going back to where it came from," Lady Blurdell explained. "The thieves in the government had less money, and much of it went back in, where hopefully some of it managed to find its way into actually helping the country. Of course, the bloodsuckers took some of the money right back, so we just had to take it from them again the next year."

"It was rather fun," Lord Blurdell mused. "But every now and then there was somebody– someone from the government who would ask us about what was going on. It happened immediately. That's when I realized. English "gentlemen" hate to pry into people's personal scandals. Perhaps it's because they're afraid someone else will start asking about their own private affairs. And I do mean "affairs." So what better way to silence questions than to imply that these people who died were terrible people we couldn't bear to talk about?"

"Surely you didn't have to carve those words on their graves?" I wondered.

"Actually, that was the icing on the cake," Lord Blurdell grinned. "Whenever some official started inquiring, we'd show them to the headstones. When they saw those graves, they figured that something absolutely awful had happened in the deceased people's pasts, and being well-trained since birth to avoid other people's unpleasantness, they said their goodbyes pretty quickly. They figured that if I were to allow those words to be carved on a headstone, then the story must be too shocking for human ears. The looks on their faces! I've lost count of all the times I had to bite my tongue to keep from laughing! The first time a tax employee saw "She will not be mourned," his pince-nez fell off in shock and shattered on the stone!"

"But something went wrong two years ago," Holmes countered. "That's why you had to buy more expensive gravestones."

"The local memorialist was in the graveyard for an aunt's headstone being installed, and he saw the four cheap stones. "Why didn't you come to me?" he asked. He knew something was wrong by our faces. So we bought a nice, big gravestone from him the next year to keep him quiet. The next year he dropped more hints, saying he got paid by the letter. So my wife wrote that little poem, bought that huge slab of rock, just to keep him happy. It cut into our profits a bit, but not too much. This year– you saw what we ordered. I don't mind. We're spreading the wealth around to people who need it. The memorialist lost two brothers and three of his seven children in the war. That's a reason why he drinks so much. I don't fault him."

"Why did you have all the "relatives" die on Christmas?"

"We came up with a story about a Canadian branch of the families. Ne'er-do-wells who married or gambled or otherwise connived their way into considerable fortunes, and after leaving England as expatriates, they wanted to be buried back home. We said they had interests in the Yukon gold fields, but the mail there only came out rarely, and as they'd died in cabins in the middle of nowhere, no one knew exactly when they'd died, but we just said Christmas for convenience, as that was about the time we'd receive a news update from our Canadian family members. We'd learn about their death on Christmas, so we'd say it just to have a date. People understood. Plus, we could claim that we'd held the memorial service when all the family was here for the holiday. No one else wants to come to a funeral at Christmastime. It was an easy way to keep the burials quiet."

"What do you intend to do now?" Holmes asked.

"Why, exactly what we've been doing," Lord Blurdell explained. His demeanor had changed. The beaten, embarrassed man was gone. "We're not going to stop. This is just compensation for the loss of our sons. And you won't tell anybody. Otherwise we'll provoke a scandal that will bring down the government. Given what we know, we'll never see a day in prison."

"We can't let this continue!" I blustered.

"You don't have a choice." Lord Blurdell had regained his backbone. "This is rough justice, and we're not going to back down just because you have qualms about a little justified extortion."

"No, you won't!" Duncan yelled. "This is wrong, and you taught me to always do the right thing. I'm ashamed of you both!"

This started a huge argument. The three Blurdells all forgot that Holmes and I were there as they launched into a no-holds barred shouting match. Father, mother, and son all screamed and fought, losing all sense of decorum and hearing none of what Holmes and I were saying.

After ten minutes, I can only explain what happened next as a true Christmas miracle. The butler pushed open the library doors, muttering, "Your lordship. Your ladyship. I can't believe it..." Behind him limped a young man. He was gaunt, haggard, and looked as if every step caused him great pain. But the sight of him had an incredible effect on the Blurdells.

"Timmy!"

"Timmy?"

"My God! My son!"

The long-lost son gulped down a little brandy, and soon told his amazing story. He had been captured in the waning days of the war in Asia, and an enemy agent who resembled him superficially had been recruited to assume his identity. Apparently he had been killed soon after embarking on his mission, and his body had been mistaken as Timmy's due to the identification papers. Meanwhile, Timmy had languished in prison, not knowing what had happened or even that the war had ended. Due to all sorts of oversights and inefficiency, he hadn't been released for many years, and the government, thinking he was dead, hadn't made efforts to rescue him. When he was finally released a month ago without money or identification papers, he was compelled to beg until he had enough to buy a steerage ticket on a ship headed home. He would have sent a telegram, but he had no funds. He'd picked up some tropical disease in prison, anyway, and spent most of his days aboard the ship in a mild state of delirium. I examined him, and though he was in poor health, after proper treatment and plenty of rest, there was no reason why he shouldn't make a full recovery.

There is little more to say. Holmes spoke to Mycroft to apprise him of the situation. Over the coming months, there were a great many resignations from the government. I was not made privy to the details, but I assumed that the Blurdells went unpunished in exchange for their silence. Apparently, the Blurdells' thirst for vengeance faded with the knowledge that one of their lost sons had survived. The family wasn't whole, but it was happier.

Young Duncan was the happiest of all, and he wasn't the least bit upset that he was no longer the heir to the family fortune. His brother's survival was more than enough for him, and I was delighted for Duncan and Timmy. Duncan had tried to give the watch he'd inherited from his other brother to Timmy, who refused it, and they eventually agreed to share the watch, though the details weren't clear. In a letter I received shortly after New Year's, Duncan told me how he and his family had celebrated the coming of 1926. That night, the Blurdells, with the help of some members of the staff, had taken eight gravestones and hurled them into a lake on the estate. Seven of the headstones were the ones with bitter epitaphs. The eighth was Timmy's. I am told that the cheering was deafening as the stone bust on Timmy's grave marker sank beneath the water.

www.ingramcontent.com/pod-product-compliance
Lightning Source LLC
Chambersburg PA
CBHW070005260626
47159CB00005B/1681